HARDY BOYS

Clue Book

4 books in 1!

HARDY BOYS

Clue Book

4 books in 1!

THE VIDEO GAME BANDIT

THE MISSING PLAYBOOK

WATER-SKI WIPEOUT

TALENT SHOW TRICKS

BY FRANKLIN W. DIXON ILLUSTRATED BY MATT DAVID

ALADDIN

NEW YORK   LONDON   TORONTO   SYDNEY   NEW DELHI

ALADDIN

An imprint of Simon & Schuster Children's Publishing Division
1230 Avenue of the Americas, New York, NY 10020
This Aladdin hardcover edition March 2019
The Video Game Bandit text copyright © 2016 by Simon & Schuster, Inc.
The Missing Playbook text copyright © 2016 by Simon & Schuster, Inc.
Water-Ski Wipeout text copyright © 2016 by Simon & Schuster, Inc.
Talent Show Tricks text copyright © 2016 by Simon & Schuster, Inc.
Cover and interior illustrations copyright © 2016 by Matt David
THE HARDY BOYS and colophons are registered trademarks of Simon & Schuster, Inc.
HARDY BOYS CLUE BOOK and colophons are trademarks of Simon & Schuster, Inc.
All rights reserved, including the right of reproduction in whole or in part in any form.
ALADDIN and related logo are registered trademarks of Simon & Schuster, Inc.
For information about special discounts for bulk purchases, please contact
Simon & Schuster Special Sales at 1-866-506-1949 or business@simonandschuster.com.
The Simon & Schuster Speakers Bureau can bring authors to your live event.
For more information or to book an event contact the Simon & Schuster Speakers Bureau
at 1-866-248-3049 or visit our website at www.simonspeakers.com.
Books designed by Karina Granda
The text of this book was set in Adobe Garamond Pro.
Manufactured in the United States of America 0219 FFG
2 4 6 8 10 9 7 5 3 1
Library of Congress Control Number 2019930241
ISBN 978-1-5344-5354-8 (hc)
ISBN 978-1-4814-5054-6 (*The Video Game Bandit* eBook)
ISBN 978-1-4814-5179-6 (*The Missing Playbook* eBook)
ISBN 978-1-4814-5057-7 (*Water-Ski Wipeout* eBook)
ISBN 978-1-4814-5182-6 (*Talent Show Tricks* eBook)
These titles were previously published individually.

CONTENTS

THE VIDEO GAME BANDIT

A PARTY FOR CHAMPIONS

"This way, over here!" Frank Hardy called out. He waved his arms back and forth, signaling his younger brother, Joe. Joe walked across the backyard with a stack of folding chairs. They were kind of heavy, and his face was beet red after carrying them over to Frank and their friend Ellie Freeman.

Frank and Joe's baseball team, the Bayport Bandits, was having a big fund-raiser. They were hoping to go to Florida on a team trip and play a few friendly games with other teams. In between games the team would be at the beach, snorkeling, paddleboarding, and learning how to surf.

Ellie's parents had volunteered to host the fundraiser at their house. They had a big backyard, where they would auction off prizes in honor of the Bayport baseball team. People from all over town had donated things for the auction—a meal at Chez Jean, the fanciest French restaurant in Bayport, sailing lessons, art classes, and a shopping spree at Blair's Boutique, a cute new store in town.

"What do you need next?" Joe asked Ellie. He dropped the metal chairs on the ground with a clatter.

"I think we need to get the tablecloths from my mom," Ellie said. She was busy unfolding another stack of chairs and setting them up in a straight line. The stage in the backyard was already assembled, and now they were figuring out where the guests would sit during the auction. A big van from Forks and Knives was parked near the side door of Ellie's house, and the workers were busy shuttling delicious-looking food from the van into the house. "This party is going to be the best in Bayport history," Frank said, looking at the decorations they'd just hung up. There were lights and streamers strung across the yard. "Do you think we'll raise enough to go to Florida?"

"You bet." Ellie grinned. "The tickets alone will give our fund a huge boost. Then we have the prizes that will be auctioned off and the fashion show—all the boutiques donated clothing just to be part of it."

"Sounds like we'll be in Florida in no time," Joe laughed. He unfolded a chair and set it down next to one of Ellie's.

With twenty-five kids on the team, it would be expensive to fly everyone down and have them stay at a hotel. They'd already had a bake sale and a car wash. With this huge event, everyone was hoping they would raise all the money they needed to bring every member of the team to Florida for free—or at least to pay for everyone's plane ticket.

As Frank and Joe helped Ellie set up the rest of

the chairs, Mrs. Freeman came out, followed by Phil Cohen, a friend from school. He was carrying a small speaker that he put down by the side of the stage. "You guys remember my friend Biff, right?" Phil asked. He pointed over his shoulder.

A tall blond boy came out of the house with the other speaker. He was wearing a blue T-shirt with the word TIGERS written across it in orange script. Right behind him was a basset hound puppy with long, floppy ears, who scampered down the stairs, tail wagging.

"Hey, guys!" Biff called. "Long time no see!"

Before Frank or Joe could even respond, the puppy jumped up on them. Frank crouched down as the puppy covered his face with wet kisses.

Biff ran over, grabbing the back of the puppy's collar. "Come on, Sherlock! Down!" he commanded.

"Sorry, he's still learning," Biff apologized.

"That's okay," Frank said, rubbing the puppy's head. "He's great."

"Sherlock?" Ellie asked, kneeling beside them. She kissed the puppy on the nose. "That's so cute."

Phil looked at his friend. "Biff and Sherlock are staying with me for the weekend while Biff's parents are away. He's helping me set up the music for the fund-raiser this afternoon," he said. "I figured we could use an extra hand."

"Isn't that nice of him?" Mrs. Freeman said as she darted past. She put a stack of tablecloths on one of the tables. "It's true, we could use all the help we can get."

"I just hope this guy doesn't cause too much trouble," Biff said, rubbing Sherlock's head. He looked down at the dog. "You're going to be a good boy, aren't you, Sherlock? Aren't you?"

"Let's hope!" Mrs. Freeman said.

Sherlock sprinted across the lawn, his ears flying up behind him. He grabbed a branch that had fallen from a nearby tree and started chewing it. As

Frank and Joe helped Ellie with the tablecloths, Phil and Biff went to work on the sound system. Frank looked over at Biff, trying to remember the last time he'd seen him. Phil had been friends with him for a long time, but Biff didn't go to the same school as they did. Frank and Joe usually only hung out with him at Phil's birthday parties every year.

Just then Mr. Freeman came around the side of the house. Mr. Fun, the owner of the local arcade, was right behind him. "Look who I found outside!" Mr. Freeman said. "Mr. Fun came to drop off his prizes for the auction."

All of them stopped what they were doing when they saw what Mr. Fun had brought. "Is that what I think it is?" Phil Cohen asked excitedly. He studied the box in Mr. Fun's hand. He was holding a ZCross5000, a video game system that had just come out the month before. *Every* kid at Bayport Elementary wanted one.

"The ZCross5000!" Mr. Fun said. "You bet it is! I waited in line at the store for five hours the day it came out. Then I came home, only to find out

Mrs. Fun had already gotten me one for my birthday. Figured you guys could use the extra for the auction. Oh . . . and these!" He held up some free passes to Fun World, his arcade.

Frank and Joe grinned. Mr. Fun had given them a whole stack once, after they'd solved a mystery at the arcade. They were known around Bayport for helping people find missing pets, stolen bikes, or even jewelry. Just a month before, they'd helped figure out who had played a prank on their good friend Chet Morton.

"This is going to be the highlight of the auction!" Mr. Freeman exclaimed. "I heard every store is sold out of the ZCross5000 now."

"They are!" Mr. Fun said. "I hope this helps the team get to Florida."

Mrs. Freeman and Ellie had climbed onto the stage. They unrolled a large banner that said THANK YOU FOR SUPPORTING THE BAYPORT BANDITS! The

Freemans had put large wooden posts in the ground, and Mrs. Freeman and Ellie hung the banner in between the posts. Ellie took a few steps back, trying to get it in just the right spot. "How does it look?" she finally asked.

"Perfect," Joe said. They all stood there, staring at the backyard. All the chairs were set up in rows now. With the decorations they had already put up, the backyard was looking great. Mrs. Freeman had even put floating candles in the pool, which looked pretty fancy.

"This is going to be so much fun," Mrs. Freeman said as she taped the banner in place. "And with a little luck, we'll have enough in the fund to send all of you to Florida for lots of baseball and sunshine!"

Frank wrapped an arm around his brother. "Soon we'll be at the beach, catching some waves!"

"Or snorkeling," Ellie chimed in.

"Or playing beach volleyball," Joe added.

Frank smiled. "Or—"

"Let's not get excited just yet!" Mr. Freeman said.

He waved for them to go back inside. "There's still work to do. We have to set up all the trays for appetizers. We need to organize the buffet table. And you three need to change into your Bayport Bandits shirts before the guests get here."

He pointed to Frank, Joe, and Ellie. They headed inside, Phil, Biff, and Sherlock following behind them.

Frank leaned toward his brother. "Not get excited?" he whispered. "That's impossible!"

LET THE BIDDING START!

"Would you like to try a coconut shrimp?" Joe held the silver tray high in the air. A woman with stiff white hair picked up a shrimp and put it on her plate. Onstage, the fashion show was in full swing. Cissy Zermeño stood in the center and did a twirl. She wore a pink dress with a wide-brimmed white hat.

"Thank you so much, Cissy!" Mrs. Freeman announced. She stood at the edge of the stage, reading from a stack of note cards. "Again, her outfit was from Lulu's Corner."

Just then their gym teacher, Mrs. Kingsman, walked across the stage in a green plaid suit. "Mrs. Kingsman is wearing a crisp Weathersby suit from Blair's Boutique," Mrs. Freeman announced. "The jacket is cropped at the waist and has tortoiseshell buttons. She's wearing it with a white ruffled blouse. Perfect for work or a business dinner. Doesn't she look sharp!"

The crowd applauded as Mrs. Kingsman strode down the steps and into the house. The fashion show had been going on for about half an hour. Miss Swivel, who worked in the Bayport Elementary School's cafeteria, modeled a long blue parka. Everyone laughed when their art teacher, Mr. Hendricks, came onstage wearing a bright orange sweater and furry hat.

"And now for our last model before we start the auction," Mrs. Freeman said. "Give a round of applause for . . . Principal Green!"

The crowd cheered as Principal Green stepped onto the stage. Most of the Bayport Bandits were weaving in and out of the audience in their baseball T-shirts, passing out appetizers. Ellie, Joe, and Frank put their trays down on a nearby table to clap for their principal. She was one of the Bayport Bandits' biggest fans.

Principal Green spun around in the center of the stage and smiled. Her dark hair was curled like she was going to a fancy ball. "Principal Green is wearing a purple polka-dot skirt with a gray silk blouse from Blair's Boutique. Doesn't she look lovely!"

Principal Green waved to the Bandits before she headed off the stage. As the audience watched the show, Frank and Joe walked through the crowd, picking up crumpled napkins and empty plates. Ellie passed out a tray of tiny hot dogs, giving a few extra to Sherlock. The puppy was wandering around the lawn, a Bandits bandanna tied around his neck. Every now and then he'd stop to beg for food or tear apart one of the paper plates that had fallen on the ground.

Phil pressed a few buttons on the sound system, and music filled the air. There were a ton of people in Ellie's backyard. Some were sitting at tables, eating the last of their food. Others sipped their drinks and talked about the fashion show. Everyone seemed excited that they could find the outfits in local stores.

Ellie found Joe as he was giving away the last of his shrimp. "Can you believe it?" she asked. "The party is a total success so far!"

"Everyone seems really happy to be here," Joe agreed.

"I just heard a group by the pool talking about the auction. One man wants to bid on the ZCross5000 for his grandson. He doesn't care how much it costs," Ellie added with a huge smile.

"Get your paddles ready!" Joe said, pretending he was the announcer. "The bidding starts in five minutes!"

Ellie and Joe were raising their hands, pretending to bid on different items, when Frank waved to them from across the lawn. "Guys! Over here!" He pointed at the photo booth set up by Ellie's old swing set. Mr. and Mrs. Freeman had hired someone to take pictures of all the guests.

Ellie and Joe crammed inside with Frank as the flash went off. It went off again and again. Ellie, Joe, and Frank made funny faces for the camera, wearing some of the props in the booth. There was a crown, a big pair of glasses, and all kinds of unique hats. They were having so much fun, they hardly noticed when the music stopped and Coach Quinn came onstage to start the auction.

"The first prize up for auction is a cooking lesson with Chef Jolene, of Jolene's Bistro!" she called out. "The bidding starts at fifty dollars."

A woman with red hair raised her paddle, which meant she wanted the lesson. But almost as soon as she did that, another woman raised her paddle. That meant the price would be higher because she wanted the lesson too. The women kept bidding against each other until the red-haired woman won.

"Going once . . . going twice . . . sold for eighty

dollars!" Coach Quinn called out. Cissy—or Speedy, as most people called her—was the pitcher for the Bandits. Everyone called her Speedy because she did everything super-fast, from talking to pitching her famous fastball! She had changed out of her fashion show outfit and was now in charge of bringing out the prizes. When she came onto the stage with a certificate for the cooking class, everyone cheered.

Frank and Joe sat by the pool as Coach Quinn auctioned off the other prizes. There were sailing lessons, art classes, and a gift certificate for a month's worth of free ice cream from the new ice cream shop in town, Two Spoons. Mrs. Zermeño, Cissy's mom, ended up bidding on a spa weekend. Mr. Carson, the woodshop teacher, had donated a hand-carved chair that went for a lot of money.

"Sold to the man in the gray hat!" Coach Quinn called out. Cissy moved the wooden chair to the right of the stage and put a red tag on it that said SOLD. Then she disappeared inside, looking for the next prize.

Coach Quinn smiled at the audience. "Thank you so much for your support today. You've all been so generous with this auction. Now I'd like to announce the last prize up for bidding. Everyone in town has been talking about the ZCross5000, the new gaming system from MegaKidz. But not many people have been playing it—the gaming system has been sold out for over a month, and it's hard to find. Today we're putting one up for auction, thanks to Mr. Fun from Fun World."

The crowd clapped. A few boys in the front row stuck their fingers in their mouths and whistled loudly. "Yeah! The ZCross5000 rocks!" one yelled.

Coach Quinn looked toward the house, waiting for Cissy to come out with the prize. A minute passed, then another. She made a few jokes to keep the audience's attention, but that only worked for so long.

"Cissy?" Coach Quinn said into the microphone. "Are you there? Will you bring out our next prize? The ZCross5000?"

Just then Cissy appeared at the back door. Her cheeks were bright red, and she looked like she might cry. Mrs. Freeman ran to her, trying to figure out what was going on. "Cissy, what is it?" Mrs. Freeman asked. "What's wrong?"

Cissy crossed her arms over her chest. "The ZCross5000 . . . Someone took it. It's gone!"

A SINGLE CLUE

"This has to be a mistake," Mrs. Freeman exclaimed. "Who would steal something from us? Who would do that?"

She looked back at the crowd, noticing that everyone was still watching Cissy and her. A few women in the front row were whispering to one another. An older man with white hair looked shocked.

Coach Quinn grabbed the microphone. "If you could excuse us, we'll need to put the auction on hold while we figure this out. In the meantime, please enjoy the dessert table!" She pointed to the other side of the patio, where a table with cookies and cakes was set up. Slowly everyone got out of their seats. Some people were still looking at Cissy and wondering what had happened.

"Do you really think someone took it?" Joe said, turning to his brother.

"I don't know," Frank replied. "Let's go see."

Cissy and Mrs. Freeman had already disappeared inside the house. Frank and Joe found them in the den. Mr. Fun was there too, along with Mr. Freeman.

"It was right here," Cissy repeated. She pointed to a spot on the floor. "I left it with some of the other prizes."

Frank and Joe scanned the den. There was a long couch, a coffee table, and a television set. In one corner was Ellie's piano, and in another was a polka-dot beanbag chair. A few family photos were on display, but other than that, the walls were bare.

"Oh, good." Mr. Fun turned around, noticing for

the first time that Frank and Joe had come inside. "You're here! What do the two best detectives in Bayport think?"

Joe was about to respond, but then he noticed Frank. His brother was on the other side of the coffee table. He knelt down and picked up a few sheets of paper. "Instructions for the ZCross5000," he whispered.

Joe walked over to get a better look. The paper booklet was ripped down the center. It looked crumpled around the edges, too. "Maybe whoever took the ZCross dropped this on their way out," Joe said.

"They were probably in a hurry," Frank added. "They definitely opened the box."

"There aren't any other signs of it, though," Joe pointed out.

"Could this be a mistake?" Mrs. Freeman asked. She kept

rubbing her temples with her fingers. "Maybe someone accidentally took it."

"I don't think so. It had a sign on it that said 'For the Auction.'" Cissy shook her head. "I saw it about half an hour ago. A few of the bigger prizes were in here, but most of the other stuff was in the dining room. I don't know what happened."

"I can't believe this," Mr. Fun said. "Whoever is responsible must be caught. They can't just walk away with it! It's maddening!"

"We'll figure out who did this," Frank promised. He scanned the room again, checking to see if there was anything they might have missed.

"I hope so," Mrs. Freeman said. She glanced out the window, where the party was still going on. "The auction was supposed to be over around five o'clock, but I don't know how long people will stay if we can't even find the biggest auction prize."

Joe pulled his notebook from his back pocket and flipped to a clean page. "There's no time to waste, then," he said. "Let's get started."

THE FIVE WS

Joe wrote *The Five Ws* at the top of the page and underlined it twice. Whenever they were trying to solve a mystery, they started with a few simple questions. He wrote *Who?*, *What?*, *Where?*, *When?*, and *Why?* underneath the heading.

"Let's start with a possible motive," Frank said. "Why would someone want to take the ZCross5000?"

Mr. Fun laughed out loud. "Well, that's easy!

Because it's a ZCross5000! Who *wouldn't* want to take it?"

"I'm afraid Mr. Fun is right," Mrs. Freeman said. "Everyone in Bayport—not to mention the whole country—wants one."

Frank walked the length of the room. "Because it's expensive and they could sell it. Because they wanted one for themselves. Because they couldn't get it anywhere else. Those are three possible motives."

Joe wrote all three down. Frank and Joe's dad, Fenton Hardy, was a private investigator. He'd taught them all about motive, which was just another way of saying why someone would do something. Every crime had to have a motive, and sometimes the motive helped you find the suspect.

"How many guests are at the party?" Joe asked.

"About a hundred," Mrs. Freeman answered. She sat down on the couch and crossed her arms over her chest. "I'm so upset. What a horrible ending to the afternoon."

"It's not over yet. Is there anyone here that you think might do something like this?" Joe asked.

Mrs. Freeman shook her head.

Suddenly Mr. Fun snapped his fingers. "Wait, I remember—I did see someone."

Joe put his pen to the paper, ready to copy down everything Mr. Fun said.

"At the beginning of the party," Mr. Fun went on, "there was a girl hanging around the den and the dining room, by the prizes. She kept looking into the other rooms, like she was searching for something. She seemed really suspicious."

Frank glanced at his brother. Most of the guests had spent the afternoon outside. It was strange that the girl had been in the house, and even stranger that she was exploring all the rooms. "Do you remember what she looked like?"

"She had a purple shirt with polka dots on and a pink streak in her hair. Her hair was brown. I think. I'm not sure."

Joe scribbled some notes. He wrote *Pink streak in hair, purple shirt with polka dots*, then a few notes

about where she'd been in the house. "Is there anyone else who might have done it? Anyone else you
can think of?"

Mr. Freeman pointed to the closed door on the
other side of the room. He lowered his voice when
he spoke. "The kitchen is right there. Do you think
one of the workers from Forks and Knives might
have taken it?"

"I don't think so, Ed," Mrs. Freeman said. "They

wouldn't. Besides, we've had them work for us at other parties. Why would they suddenly start stealing things now?"

Mr. Freeman nodded. "You have a point, but there were two or three people working in the kitchen today. Even if one of them didn't take it . . . maybe they saw something strange. If anyone used the kitchen door that goes outside, the workers would've noticed, right?"

Mrs. Freeman looked like she might argue with him, so Frank jumped in. "We'll question them just in case. It helps to have witnesses, too."

Joe looked at Cissy. "You said that you saw the ZCross here just half an hour ago?" he asked.

Cissy looked uncertain. "I think it was half an hour ago, but then again . . . I'm not sure. I thought I saw it at the beginning of the auction, whenever that was."

"I think the auction started right at three o'clock," Mrs. Freeman added. She pointed to Joe's notebook, as if to say, *You should probably write that down.*

"So the ZCross could've disappeared anywhere between three o'clock and now—four fifteen." Frank plopped down in the beanbag chair, deep in thought.

Joe wrote down *Between 3:00 p.m. and 4:15 p.m.* under *When?* He wrote *ZCross5000* under *What?* That was always the easiest question to answer. *Where?* was simple too. The ZCross had been taken from the Freemans' den, where it was waiting to be auctioned off.

"I really don't think the workers had anything to do with it," Mrs. Freeman repeated.

"Don't worry," Joe said, looking at the list. "We'll figure out what happened. We should start by talking to the girl Mr. Fun mentioned."

Frank stood and peered out the back window and into the yard. There were a bunch of people around the side of the stage, looking at the prizes from the auction. Guests were still using the photo booth. Some were huddled around the dessert table, piling cookies onto their plates. It was a huge crowd of people, and Frank didn't see a girl in a purple shirt anywhere.

"We just have to find her," he said. "And we don't have much time."

Joe joined him, scanning the crowd. "Agreed. But where should we start?"

PICTURE PERFECT

Joe squeezed through the crowd, moving around toward the pool. There was a group of kids he didn't recognize. He thought they might've been some of Ellie's friends from camp. He looked at each of the girls' outfits, but none of them matched the description Mr. Fun had given.

"Have you seen a girl with a purple shirt and a streak in her hair?" Joe asked a blond boy with glasses.

The boy just shrugged. "A streak? What do you mean?"

"Her hair was colored—she had pink in it," Joe explained.

The boy shook his head. A few of the other girls were playing tag on the lawn. They stopped for a moment, watching Joe. "I think I saw someone like that, but I don't know her name," a girl with braces said.

"Do you remember where?" Joe asked.

"No, just that she was here at the party somewhere," the girl explained. "Sorry."

Joe had wasted almost twenty minutes walking around in circles, trying to find the girl Mr. Fun had mentioned. He was starting to wonder if she actually existed. He'd checked all the rooms in the house, making sure she wasn't hiding somewhere. He'd looked at the tables by the pool and studied the groups of people sitting on the chairs by the stage. He'd even gone to the edge of the woods behind the backyard, where Ellie's old playhouse was.

He spotted Frank across the lawn, by the dessert

table. "Did you find anything?" Frank called out.

"Nothing," Joe said. He walked over and picked up a chocolate chip cookie. "Maybe she already left."

"Look," Frank said, pointing to the photo booth across the way. "Are you thinking what I'm thinking?"

"It couldn't hurt to check," Joe said. "There's a chance she might've taken a picture there. We might find some more clues."

The boys took off across the lawn, waiting in line while Cissy's parents posed in front of a background with the Bayport Bandits logo. "Looking good!" the man behind the camera said. "Let's see your big smiles!"

Mrs. Zermeño held a feathered fan and wore a floppy hat with ribbons on it, and Mr. Zermeño had goofy sunglasses on. They both looked nervous. They straightened up as soon as they saw Frank and Joe. "Did you find anything? What happened?" Mrs. Zermeño asked, turning to the boys.

"Nothing yet," Frank said.

Joe went over to the man behind the camera. He was a tall, skinny guy with suspenders and a fedora. He had his laptop computer on the table in front of him. With a few clicks of the mouse, he printed out copies of the pictures of Mr. and Mrs. Zermeño. They didn't look very happy in any of the pictures.

"Let us know if we can help with anything. This is just terrible," Mrs. Zermeño said, before walking off.

"You want to take another turn in the booth?" the guy asked. "I'll be closing it up in a little bit."

"Actually, we were hoping you could help us with something," Frank explained. "Do you keep all the pictures on your computer?"

"Yeah," the guy said. "Just about. Unless someone really hates the photo and wants me to delete it. But eventually they all go up on the website the day after the party."

Joe glanced sideways at his brother, knowing they were onto something. "Can we see them? We're looking for a girl who had a pink streak in her hair. We were hoping she stopped by here."

"That sounds familiar," the guy said. He clicked through screen after screen of photos. Finally he stopped on a set of four. Sure enough, they were pictures of a girl in a purple shirt with brown hair. One piece in the front was dyed pink.

"That's definitely her—she matches the description," Joe added.

The guy hit print, and a strip of four photos came out. "Here, so you have it."

Joe and Frank studied the pictures. In them, the girl in the purple shirt was next to a girl with short blond hair. Freckles covered her nose and cheeks. She looked a year or two younger than the girl with the short hair—maybe she was eight or nine. They were making angry punk-rock faces in two of the photos, and silly faces in the others.

"Thanks for this," Frank said. "Now we have something to show people."

"I don't think I saw either of them," Joe whispered as they scanned the crowd.

"Me neither," Frank added. They pushed past a group of teachers who were talking about the fashion show. Principal Green was in the center of them, making a joke about the furry orange hat Mr. Hendricks had to wear.

The boys checked the backyard again. They checked the patio and the playhouse. It wasn't until they went back to the dessert table that they spotted her. The freckle-faced girl was there alone, taking a bite of chocolate cake.

"Can we talk to you?" Joe asked, walking up to her. "We were hoping you could tell us who your friend is."

The girl's green eyes widened. "Where'd you get those?" she asked, looking at the strip of pictures. "Those are mine."

Before Joe could answer, she plucked the photos from his hand. "We've been looking for your friend," he said.

"Why?" the girl asked. "We aren't friends. Where'd you find these?"

"The guy from the picture booth gave them to us," Frank explained. "What do you mean, you aren't friends?"

"Never mind," the girl with freckles said. Frank was about to ask her more, but the girl turned on her heel and headed across the lawn, to where the other kids were playing tag.

"That was really weird," Joe whispered.

"Really weird," Frank agreed. "Why would they take pictures together if they aren't friends?"

As they stood there, watching her join the game of tag, they were more confused than ever.

"She's hiding something," Joe finally said. "The only question is what."

A SECRET IN THE WOODS

Frank and Joe were still standing there, confused, when a little boy with red hair and freckles came up to them. He had chocolate around his mouth. He couldn't have been more than six or seven years old.

"Do you guys know my sister, Lisi?" he said. He pointed to the girl with the freckles. She was running across the grass, reaching out to tag a boy with curly black hair.

"Kind of," Frank said. It wasn't a lie . . . not really.

"Have you met her friend with the pink streak in her hair?" Joe asked.

"Kendall," the little boy said. "But Mom and Dad said they weren't allowed to hang out anymore. They always get in trouble when they're together."

Joe raised his eyebrows at his brother. No wonder Lisi had been so nervous when she saw the pictures of them together. She probably hadn't realized they would be on the website, or that anyone else would see them. If she wasn't allowed to hang out with Kendall, the pictures might get her in trouble.

"Do you know where we could find Kendall?" Frank asked.

The little boy shrugged. "I don't know . . . she was here before. My mom says Kendall likes doing her own thing. What does that mean?"

Joe scratched his head. It might have seemed like a small detail, but it would definitely help them. He and Frank had spent the last half hour looking in all the most crowded places. Maybe they should have been looking in the quiet rooms of the house, or the places no one else would go.

"I have an idea," Joe said, waving for Frank to follow him. They thanked the boy as they headed off to the back of the yard, where the woods began.

"Where are we going?" Frank asked.

"To the quietest place there is," Joe said. "Ellie's old tree house. I walked around it before, but I never looked inside."

"Good thinking," Frank said. He followed Joe, his feet crunching down on dry leaves and twigs. Soon they could see the tree house through the trees. It was dirty, and all the shutters were closed.

When they got there, Joe knocked on the tiny door. "Kendall? Are you there?"

One of the shutters opened, and the girl with the pink streak in her hair peered out. "Who's asking?"

"We just have a few questions for

you," Frank said. "Someone saw you in the Freemans' house around the time the ZCross went missing. Did you see anything strange?"

"Ugh," Kendall sighed. She closed the shutter and opened the door, letting them in. Frank and Joe both had to duck a little to walk around. They noticed she had a sketchbook. She was drawing different objects in the house—an old plastic teapot and some broken crayons.

"I hope you didn't tell my mom I'm back here," she huffed.

"No," Joe said. "We don't even know who your mom is."

"We did talk to Lisi," Frank said. "Are you two friends?"

Kendall laughed. "Yeah, just don't tell her parents that. That's why I was in Ellie's house before. Lisi and I had a plan to hang out during the fashion show, when her mom wouldn't notice. She's still upset over this expensive vase we broke the last time I went over to their house. It was a total accident! I tripped and fell!"

"So you were in the house during the fashion show? Where?" Joe asked.

"We actually stayed on the front porch, playing Spit. You know that card game?" Kendall said.

"Who won?" Frank asked.

"Lisi did—she's pretty good." Kendall sat down on the floor of the playhouse and crossed her legs. She closed her sketchbook and put it in her lap.

"Did you see anything suspicious?" Joe said.

"Nope. You can ask Lisi, too, if you want—she was with me the whole time." Kendall twisted the piece of pink hair around her finger. "Is that it? I want to finish my drawing before the party ends."

Joe looked at his older brother, wondering if they were thinking the same thing. Kendall seemed to be telling the truth. She hadn't even paused when Frank asked her who won the card game.

"I think that's it," Frank said.

"Let us know if you remember anything else," Joe added before they left.

When they were far enough away from the

playhouse, Frank finally spoke. "I think she's telling the truth," he said.

"Me too," Joe agreed. "Which means our only other lead is the workers Mr. Freeman mentioned."

Frank sped up, walking faster back to the party. "Let's talk to them as soon as we can," he said. "Everyone will be leaving soon—we're running out of time."

TOO MANY COOKS

As Joe and Frank made their way back to the house, they noticed the party was quieter than before. A lot of guests had left. Phil had abandoned the stereo, putting on music that sounded like what you'd hear in an elevator.

"Mrs. Freeman seemed pretty sure the people who helped set up the party didn't have anything to do with it," Joe said. "If they've worked at other parties at Ellie's house, it doesn't make sense that they'd suddenly walk in and take the ZCross. What would be the point of that?"

"It's our only lead now," Frank said. "We have to follow it."

Their dad had taught them about leads, which were clues that pointed the investigator in a certain direction. This one was leading them to the people who worked for Forks and Knives. There was a reason Mr. Freeman had mentioned them, and they had to explore it. As they walked into the kitchen, they tried to stay hopeful. Maybe Mr. Freeman was right. Maybe the workers *did* know something about the missing ZCross.

A man with a white bandanna around his head was washing dishes. A few other people brought trays in from outside. Frank, Joe, and the rest of the Bandits had met all the workers at the beginning of the party. For most of the event the Bandits had been going inside and picking up appetizers, then passing them out to all the guests.

A blond woman was arranging a plate of giant brownies. She looked up when Frank and Joe walked in. "Can I help you?" she asked.

"We were hoping to talk to you about the missing video game system—the ZCross everyone's been looking for."

The woman sprinkled some powdered sugar on the brownies. "Wish I knew more, but I didn't see anything. What about you, Larry?"

The man with the bandanna shrugged. "Nothing."

Joe pulled out his notepad, hoping a few questions might help them remember something. "Did you notice anyone go into the den from the kitchen? Or maybe they came out of the den? We think whoever took it would have left this way—otherwise they would have had to go through the backyard."

The woman had a white jacket that said HEATHER on the front in curly script. She pulled a lemon custard pie from the fridge. "I didn't, but I was busy prepping the desserts."

Just then a teenage girl came into the room. She looked like she went to Bayport High School. She had her hair in a ponytail and was wearing a shirt that said FORKS AND KNIVES. She put a pile of dirty dishes into the sink and turned to go.

"Excuse us!" Joe called out. "Did you see anything strange this afternoon? We're trying to figure out who took the ZCross from the den. We still haven't been able to find it."

The girl threw up her hands. "I just told Christina, but she didn't think it meant anything!" She laughed.

Heather and the man with the bandanna both turned, suddenly interested. "What do you mean?" Joe asked.

"I saw two kids right before the auction. They came out of the den. They both had something under their shirts. They were practically running out the front door." The girl put her hands on her hips.

Joe started writing down everything she said. "What did they look like?"

She shook her head. "I didn't get a good look, that's the problem. They were moving too fast. But the one kid . . . whatever he was holding under his shirt . . . it looked like it was alive."

"What?" Frank said loudly. "What do you mean?"

"It was squirming," the girl said.

"A boy with a squirming stomach? This is starting to sound like an alien movie." Joe laughed. He wrote it all down anyway.

"I think the other kid had the game. There were, like . . . cords and stuff coming out from under his shirt. It wasn't in the box anymore." The girl shrugged. "I don't know what else to tell you."

A boy with glasses and braces came in with another tray of dirty dishes. He set them down on the counter. It was obvious that he'd been listening to their conversation. "I saw those kids too!" he cried. Frank noticed that his name tag said KEVIN. "You're right, Alana. I was taking some dishes out to the van and saw them come out too. I heard them talking about some game, and now I realize they were probably talking about the ZCross. I didn't even realize they might've been the ones who took the ZCross."

"This has been a huge help, really," Frank said. "Do you remember what they were wearing?"

Alana pulled a stool away from the counter and plopped down. "I think one had a gray T-shirt and the other was wearing a blue one. They both had on jeans."

Kevin shook his head. "No, no—you've got it all wrong. They were wearing sweatshirts. I'm sure of it."

Alana and Kevin started arguing. Joe wasn't quite sure what to write down, so he wrote down

Blue T-shirt & gray T-shirt OR two sweatshirts under the description of the suspects. This happened a lot. Most of the time witnesses couldn't remember what the suspects looked like, or they remembered different things.

"What about their hair color or their eye color?" Frank asked.

Alana let out a sigh. "I think they both had brown hair."

Kevin shook his head again. "One was blond, don't you remember?"

Frank glanced sideways at his brother. It was clear they weren't going to get Alana and Kevin to agree on anything. "If you remember anything else, let us know. We're going to look around the den one last time and see if we missed anything."

As they left, Alana and Kevin were still arguing. "Maybe he had red hair," Alana whispered, more confused than ever. "I just don't know anymore."

Joe and Frank shut the door to the den behind them. "So two boys took the ZCross," Joe said. "That makes sense. Now we just have to figure out which two boys. Do you think we should go through the photo booth pictures again?"

"They didn't give us a good enough description," Frank said, pacing the room. "Maybe there's more here . . . there has to be something we missed."

The boys started searching the room again, this time checking the cabinet beneath the television set and the small table by the couch. Sometimes when they returned to the scene of a mystery they found smaller clues they'd missed the first time. Frank knelt down and looked under the couch, while Joe examined the crumpled ZCross pamphlet again.

"Why would someone tear it apart?" Joe asked.

Frank was leaning over the back of the couch, reaching for something there. "Why would they tear the entire box apart?" he asked.

Joe thought it was a strange question until he realized what Frank had found. There, behind the couch, was the entire ZCross box. And one whole side of it was shredded. Joe stepped closer to get a better look. But it was empty.

"It's like someone ripped it. Do you think they

were trying to get it out of the box in a hurry?"

Frank opened the end, which was kind of slimy. "Ewww . . . it's wet. Gross."

He and Joe stood there, studying the shredded box. "Maybe they were trying to avoid being seen. The game box is smaller than a giant cardboard thing," Joe said. "Maybe they were hoping no one would notice them leave."

"Still," Frank said, "they didn't have to rip the box apart. This is so strange. It makes no sense."

Joe looked out the window at the party. Whoever did this had been here, as a guest. But why would they leave evidence behind? And what was the second boy holding, the one with the squirming stomach?

For the first time ever, the Hardy Boys were seriously stumped.

FORGOTTEN EVIDENCE

"Let's see what we know so far," Joe said, plopping down on the couch next to his brother. He flipped open his notebook. "Who . . ."

Frank leaned over, looking at the page. Joe had crossed out the description Mr. Fun had given them of the girl with the purple shirt and pink streak in her hair. He'd crossed out the names Kendall and Lisi, too. Underneath he'd written:

Two boys

One held game under his shirt

One had squirming stomach

Blue T-shirt and gray T-shirt OR two sweatshirts

Both had brown hair (or maybe red?) or brown hair
and blond hair

Frank shook his head. "We don't really have much to work with," he said. "I guess we know that the boys aren't on the Bayport Bandits—otherwise they would have been wearing the same shirts we are. But besides that, these two kids could be anyone. What other clues do we have?"

Joe turned the page. "Just the other details about the ripped-up box. We're sure it's not Kendall and Lisi, right? Should we go back to them to see if they might have noticed the two boys Kevin and Alana saw?"

Before Frank could answer, there was a knock

on the den door. Kevin opened it and poked his head inside. "Um . . . I remembered one more thing!" he said, slipping in and shutting the door behind him.

Kevin sat down on a chair and started talking. "As the boys were leaving, I heard them say something about a guy named Mr. Fun. Do you think that was some kind of code?"

Joe laughed. "No, Mr. Fun is a real person. He's the owner of Fun World. You know, that arcade downtown?"

Kevin's eyes widened. "Ohhhh! Yeah, I used to go there all the time. I was obsessed with the Shooting Hoops game there."

Frank leaned in, listening closer. "Do you remember what they said about Mr. Fun?" he asked.

Kevin shook his head. Joe noticed that the front of his uniform shirt had a white smear on it. It looked like vanilla frosting. "No . . . just something about Mr. Fun. Then the one kid said, 'We could be back in half an hour.' They were going somewhere."

Joe scribbled down everything Kevin said, hoping it might be another lead. "Did they say where?"

"No," Kevin said. "They went into the garage, though. And then I didn't see them again. I still haven't seen them. But I'll tell you—I was right, one of the kids had blond hair, I swear. I don't know why Alana was arguing with me."

"Did they seem excited? Happy?" Frank asked. Maybe if they knew how the kids were acting, they'd be able to figure out why they'd taken the ZCross. It might have been that they really wanted it, just like everyone else. Or they might have had another reason.

Kevin took his glasses off and wiped them with his shirt. His eyes looked much smaller without them. "Now that you say that," he said, "they actually seemed kind of scared. Or maybe nervous? I could be wrong, but I remember thinking they didn't look like thieves."

Joe wrote down what Kevin said, including the detail about them looking scared or nervous. It was all just Kevin's opinion, not fact. Still, it was helpful to collect any information they could. "Do you remember anything else?" Joe asked.

Kevin shook his head. "I think that's it."

"We should check the garage," Joe said, turning to his brother. As Kevin went back into the kitchen, they headed there. When they got inside, through the side door, they didn't notice anything unusual. All Mr. Freeman's tools were on his workbench in the corner. Rakes, shovels, and brooms were hanging from hooks on the back wall. Mr. and Mrs. Freeman's cars weren't inside, just a few bikes the family had. Ellie's bike had a neon-pink stripe on the handlebars.

Frank looked around the garage, trying to find anything strange. "Whoever the kids were, I don't think they were interested in selling the ZCross."

Joe checked the rakes and brooms on the wall. "Why do you say that?"

"Because all of Mr. Freeman's tools are sitting right here. Power drills, electric saws . . . If they wanted to make money by selling things, wouldn't they have taken these, too?"

"Good point," Joe said, moving over to the bikes. "Bingo."

Frank turned around. "What is it? What did you find?"

Joe leaned over two of the bikes. They looked like they had just been taken out for a ride. They weren't leaning on the wall like the other two. Instead, they were in the middle of the garage and the kickstands were down. "Look right here," he said, pointing to one of the baskets.

Frank picked up the evidence to examine it. Inside a clear plastic bag were four tiny hot dogs. They were the same ones he and Joe had served the guests just a few hours before. "Do you think they took these as a snack?" Frank asked. He peered through the plastic bag at Joe.

"I don't know . . . maybe," Joe said. In the same basket was a black wallet. Joe opened it, hoping there would be clues

inside. There were a few worn baseball cards from some team called the Tigers. There was a smushed piece of bubble gum and three dollars. Joe flipped through the other compartments, hoping to find anything with a name on it, but there was nothing.

"There's not even a library card," Joe said, passing the wallet to Frank. "Nothing to tell us who it belongs to."

"Well, whoever took it, they'll come back for it," Frank said. "I doubt they'd just leave their wallet behind."

"What do you think about Mr. Fun?" Joe asked.

"I always liked Mr. Fun," Frank said, turning the wallet upside down. Two pennies fell out.

"Why would they mention him?" Joe asked. "Do you think it's just because he was the one who donated the prize?"

"Maybe," Frank said. "One thing's for certain, though. Whoever these boys are, they'll be back to get this wallet. We should be here when they do."

Joe scanned the garage. "A stakeout. That's a great idea. We'll need a place to hide, then."

The boys went to work, looking for the best spot they could find. They'd sit quietly, hidden somewhere close by, and watch. They'd wait as long as they had to. And when their two suspects returned, they'd be ready.

THE MYSTERY MAN

Joe pushed back against the workbench, trying to get comfortable. He was wedged behind a stool, his knees against his chest. Whenever he tried to move, he got stuck. "I'm squished," he said.

Frank sat beside him, his arms wrapped around his knees. "Me too. Hopefully, it won't be much longer."

They'd been sitting under the workbench for a while. They'd pulled two stools in front of them so they'd be harder to see. Ten minutes in, Joe got hot. They had to open one of the giant garage doors to let some fresh air in.

At one point Mr. Freeman had come looking for them, and Frank and Joe had let him in on the plan. The dessert table was almost empty. People were still asking about what had happened, and Mr. Freeman worried that everyone would leave before they found the ZCross. The fund-raiser was almost over.

"Come on," Joe said, tapping his toe nervously. "Where are they?"

"They'll come," Frank said. "Just wait. We're so close, I can feel it."

Joe watched the garage door, hoping one of the boys would appear outside. He leaned his head on Frank's shoulder. He was very sleepy. They'd spent the whole day getting ready for the party. With all

the excitement of the case, Joe was ready for a nap. He tried to fight it, but he could feel himself falling asleep.

Suddenly Frank poked him in his side. "Pssssst!" he whispered. "Joe, wake up! Look!"

Joe rubbed his eyes. A boy was hovering by the

garage door. He had a blue baseball cap on, and the brim was pulled down so it was hard to see his eyes. Joe squinted, trying to make out his face, but the garage was dark and it was hard to see.

Sure enough, the boy went over to the bike. He took the wallet from the basket and slipped it into his back pocket. Then he took the plastic bag with hot dogs and threw it in the trash by the workbench.

When he turned back around, Frank and Joe saw their chance. They pushed out from under the workbench. "We need to talk to you," Frank said. "We have good reason to think you took the missing ZCross5000."

The boy's back was facing Frank and Joe. He straightened up when he heard Frank's voice. Then, without saying a word, he ran out of the garage and down the street.

"Get him!" Joe cried. He took off after the boy, Frank following close behind. They ran as fast as they could. Up ahead, the boy was running even faster. He turned the corner and sprinted up the block.

Joe tried to keep up. He cut through a neighbor's yard and watched as the boy disappeared into the woods behind Ellie's house. When Frank finally caught up to Joe, Joe stopped, his hands on his knees, trying to catch his breath.

"Where did he go?" Frank asked, looking into the trees. "Did we lose him?"

"I think so," Joe said. He could hear the boy running somewhere ahead of them, but he couldn't see him anymore. He wasn't even sure which direction he'd gone. He might have been headed back to Ellie's house, but he could have cut through the woods to the pond on the other side.

Just then Joe spotted something a few yards away. He ran over to it, picking up the cap the boy had left behind. He turned it over in his hands and looked inside. The tag had a name written on it. He brought it close to his face so he could read it.

"Of course," Joe finally said. "I should have realized it was him. The clues were there all along."

"What, what is it?" Frank asked. "What did you find?"

THE HARDY BOYS—and
YOU!

CAN YOU SOLVE THE MYSTERY OF THE VIDEO GAME BANDIT?

Grab a piece of paper and write your answers down. Or just turn the page to find out!

1. Frank and Joe came up with a list of suspects. Can you think of more? List your suspects.

2. Write down the way you think the prized ZCross5000 disappeared.

3. Which clues helped you to solve this mystery? Write them down.

A VERY NAUGHTY PUPPY

"It was Biff," Joe finally said. "But why?"

Joe handed his brother the blue cap. The tag inside read BIFF. Joe still had his name written on all his clothes from camp last summer. They made you do that so they could find them in the laundry.

"We should go find Phil," Frank said. "Come on, we can get back to the house through the woods. We just have to follow the music."

The boys took off through the trees. From

somewhere up ahead, they could hear the music from the party. The noise got louder and louder as they reached the back fence. They passed the tree house where they'd found Kendall. When they reached the edge of the woods, the party was just ending. A bunch of guests were grabbing their things and starting to leave.

"Thank you all for coming today," Coach Quinn said. "We've raised a lot of money for the Bayport Bandits, and we're nearly at our goal for the baseball trip fund."

Frank and Joe ran up to Phil, who was stationed by the sound system. They didn't want to accuse him of anything, but they knew that if Biff was the one who'd taken the ZCross, Phil had likely helped him. Kevin and Alana had agreed there were two boys coming out of the den, not one.

"Phil, we need to talk to you," Frank said. "We know Biff took the ZCross. We just need to know why. Does he still have it? What happened?"

Phil's cheeks turned pale. "Uh—oh no," he stuttered.

"It's okay, Phil," Joe said. "We just want to find it. We were hoping to have it auctioned off before everyone leaves. There's not much time."

Phil sighed. "I can explain, I swear," he said. "It was all a big misunderstanding. Right after the auction started, Biff and I went inside to check on Sherlock. And when we went into the den, we saw him with the ZCross5000. He had chewed half the box, and he was about to chew the remote, too!"

"We found the box," Frank said. "So I guess that was drool all over it? Yuck!"

Phil let out a small laugh. "Yeah, and when we saw it, we kind of freaked out. We knew it was the biggest prize of the auction, and Sherlock had destroyed the box. That's when we remembered that Mr. Fun had gotten one for his birthday. We figured he might have the extra box at his house. We went there looking for it, but his son said they'd already thrown the box away."

"You could have told us," Joe said. "We would have understood."

"Well, we wanted to, but by the time we got back, everyone had already decided it was stolen. We panicked—we didn't know what to do." Phil put his face in his hands. "We should've said something . . . I realize that now."

"So the boy with the squirming stomach?" Frank said, looking at Joe. "Let me guess, did you or Biff put Sherlock under your shirt when you snuck out of the den?"

That made Phil smile. "Yeah . . . how'd you know?"

Frank didn't respond. Instead, he just laughed. "Well, maybe we can auction off the ZCross without the box. Do you still have it? Where is it?"

"Yeah," Phil said, waving for the boys to come

with him. "I think Biff was going to try to fix the old box. Come with me."

Frank and Joe followed Phil inside the house. Sure enough, when they got to the den, Biff was already there. His face was bright red, and he looked like he might cry. He had the ZCross in the package, but the box was still disgusting.

"It's no use!" he cried when he saw Phil. "It's totally messed up. We're going to get into so much—"

Before he could finish, he looked behind Phil and saw Frank and Joe there. "It's okay," Frank said. "Phil told us what happened. We're here to help. Let's talk to Coach Quinn. We might be able to auction off the ZCross even though it doesn't have the box. It's worth a try."

"We're so sorry we didn't tell anyone what happened," Phil said. "Really."

"Don't worry about it," Joe said, following Biff outside to the hall closet. He opened it. There, sitting behind some towels, was the chewed, soggy gaming system. Joe pulled it out, finally holding it in his hands. "Let's go—there's still time."

Ten minutes later Coach Quinn was back onstage. "Thank you for all your patience," she said. "We're very happy to say the ZCross5000 has been found, and it's ready for a new home! As some of you may have heard, we don't have a box for it. But I assure you it's in mint condition. The bidding starts at one hundred dollars."

Before she could even finish the sentence, three paddles in the audience went up. "Do I hear one hundred and twenty? One hundred and forty?" Coach Quinn asked. She kept raising the price, but even more paddles shot up. Everyone wanted the ZCross5000. It didn't matter whether it was in a box or not.

"This is unbelievable!" Joe exclaimed as the bidding reached three hundred dollars.

The boys watched as a woman with gray hair and an old man with glasses battled it out. Every time the woman raised her bidding paddle, the old man would raise his. After a few minutes the bidding war ended.

"Sold to the woman with the gray hair!" Coach Quinn said. Almost as soon as those words came out of her mouth, she froze. "I—I mean, sold to the woman in the blue scarf!" she stammered as everyone, including the woman, laughed. Coach Quinn laughed too. "I'm sorry, I didn't mean to be rude. I'm just so excited. That six hundred dollars will really help the Bayport Bandits get to their goal and to Florida. Thank you, everyone, and have a good night!"

The crowd clapped as the woman went up to get her prize, which Mrs. Freeman had put in a big, fancy silver gift bag. Frank put his arm around his brother, happy with how everything had turned out. They'd found the ZCross5000 and auctioned it off, and hopefully, the whole team would be going to Florida.

"We did it," Frank said, smiling. "Another case solved!"

THE MISSING PLAYBOOK

BASEBALL BARBECUE

As soon as his father pulled up to Cissy "Speedy" Zermeño's house, Joe Hardy threw open the car door and ran up to the house. Frank smiled and rolled his eyes at his eight-year-old younger brother. On the inside, though, Frank was just as excited as Joe was about the party at Speedy's. The annual Bandit Barbecue dinner meant the beginning of baseball season, his favorite time of year.

Frank grabbed the plate of brownies his mother

had made, and his parents followed him up the walkway to the Zermeños' front door. Joe had already disappeared somewhere inside, and Speedy was waiting at the door to greet them. Speedy's real name was Cissy, but she got her nickname from how quickly she did everything, from the speed of her legendary fastball to how quickly she talked.

"Hi-Mr.-and-Mrs.-Hardy-hey-Frank-come-on-in!" she said. *"I'm-so-excited-you're-here-wow-those-brownies-look-delicious!"*

"Hi, Speedy," Frank said. "How's the wrist?"

"Great!" Speedy held up her right hand. The last time Frank had seen her in school on Friday, she'd been wearing a brace. But now it was gone. *"The-doctor-said-the-sprain—"*

"Whoa, whoa!" Frank interrupted. "Slow down!"

Speedy laughed and took a deep breath before she spoke again, more slowly this time. "The doctor said my sprain is almost completely healed. He says I'll be able to pitch in our first game next week!"

"That's awesome!" Frank exclaimed. Speedy, along with the rest of the team, had been worried when she'd hurt her wrist in gym class a couple of weeks ago. She was their star pitcher, and without her, they didn't stand a chance against their rivals the Jupiters.

"*Oh-I-know!* I can't wait to pitch the first game!" Speedy said.

Frank and Mr. and Mrs. Hardy followed Speedy outside to the backyard, where the barbecue was in full swing. Mr. and Mrs. Hardy stopped to talk to the other parents, while Frank and Speedy went looking for Joe. They found him at the backyard swing set with the Mortons. Frank and Joe's best friend, Chet, was taking turns pushing his two younger sisters—Iola, who played for the Bandits, and Mimi, who went everywhere Iola did—on the swings. A camera was hanging from a strap around Chet's neck.

"Hi, Chet," Frank said. He nodded at the camera. "You taking pictures of the party?"

"Yup!" Chet said. He gave Iola a push and then grabbed his camera, holding it up for Frank to see. "There are so many cool things you can do with this camera!" He began to explain to Frank how all the different buttons worked.

"Chet!" Mimi wailed. Her swing had come to a stop because Chet, distracted by his camera, had forgotten to push her. When Chet had a new hobby, he forgot about everything else.

"Oh, sorry," he said. He gave her a big push that sent her flying up into the air.

"What's that on your back, Mimi?" Joe asked.

"My new backpack!" Mimi squealed, kicking her feet to keep the swing going. "Isn't it cool? It's got butterflies on it!"

"She's starting preschool in the fall," Iola explained. "She's barely taken that backpack off since Mom bought it for her."

"Because it's *cool*!" Mimi said.

"Well, I'm starved," Iola said, hopping off her swing. "Who wants to get a hamburger?"

Everyone else said they were hungry too, except for Chet.

"But I'll come with you guys," he said. "I want to take some pictures of the food. Coach Quinn said I could be the team's official photographer."

They all got into the line next to the grill. Speedy's dad was hard at work cooking up hamburgers and hot dogs, moving almost as fast as Speedy did. Standing in front of them in line was Tommy Dawson, who was an outfielder and relief pitcher for the Bandits, and Ezra Moore, who was new to the team.

"It's so unfair," Tommy complained to Ezra, loud enough that Frank could hear him. "I thought I was finally going to get to pitch."

"Sorry, dude," Ezra said, "but Speedy's the starting pitcher. You knew Coach Quinn was going to let her pitch as soon as her wrist was healed."

"She shouldn't be the starter anyway," Tommy said. "I'm ten

times better than she is. Coach Quinn's just got it in for me. I'm not going to let Coach get away with this."

"Tommy, calm down," Ezra said.

"No way. Forget this stupid team!" Tommy snapped. He stalked off, ignoring Ezra's attempts to stop him.

Ezra noticed Frank listening in on their conversation.

"He'll cool off," he said. "He's just disappointed."

Frank nodded. He was just glad Speedy hadn't heard what Tommy was saying.

The kids loaded up their plates with food and sat in the grass with some of the other Bandits to eat. When they were done, someone found a baseball and they started a game of catch. All the younger brothers and sisters of the Bandits players were sitting around Mimi, whose backpack was jammed full of coloring books, stuffed animals, and other toys that she was handing out. They played while the older kids tossed the ball and the parents watched, chatting as they sipped their cups of punch.

Soon it began to grow dark, and the party moved

inside. The parents gathered in the kitchen, while the little kids sat in front of the television in the living room to watch a movie. Mimi was among them, her empty backpack slung over her shoulders. While they watched the movie, most of the kids played with one of the toys or coloring books that Mimi had given them.

Meanwhile, Coach Quinn gathered all the Bandits together for a team meeting.

"Thanks for coming, everyone," she said when the team was sitting before her. "It's going to be the start of an awesome season, right?"

"Right!" they all chorused. Joe's voice was the loudest of all, Frank noticed. Coach Quinn's eyes twinkled. "That's what I thought. Now, let me show you our new secret weapon."

Chapter 2.

PRANK NIGHT

Coach Quinn pulled a bright-red notebook from her bag. It had PLAYBOOK printed across it in bold black letters. Chet's camera flashed as he took a picture.

"This is our new playbook," she explained. "I've been coming up with new training methods and batting lineups that are going to make us the best team we can be. We're going to work hard and play even harder, and then what's going to happen?"

"We're going to *win*!" Joe shouted, and the rest of the team cheered.

"And what else?" Coach Quinn asked.

"Have fun!" everyone yelled.

Coach Quinn laughed. "That's right! Now have a good time tonight, because the hard work starts tomorrow!"

The meeting over, the team members went back to the party. Frank asked Coach Quinn if he could look at the playbook, and she handed it to him. He flipped through it slowly. One section showed new drills that would help them become faster, stronger, and pitch the ball even better. Another

section had a dozen different batting orders, one for any situation they might face. Frank's eyes widened as he took it all in. He could almost feel the championship trophy in his hands.

Joe tapped on his shoulder,

interrupting his fantasy of scoring the game-winning run at the championships.

"Frank, come on," he said. "We're playing Pin the Hat on the Ballplayer in the dining room."

Frank put the playbook down on the coffee table and headed after his brother. On his way, he nearly tripped over Mimi, who was sprawled on the floor, scribbling in a coloring book.

In the dining room, Speedy's mom was leading the game. She had tied a blindfold around Ezra Moore's eyes, and he was trying to stick a paper ball cap with tape on the back to the large poster of a baseball player tacked to the wall. After feeling around for a while, Ezra stuck the cap near the ballplayer's elbow. Everyone laughed and clapped when he took off the blindfold, stomped his foot, and said, "Darn it!"

Frank was watching Mrs. Zermeño put the blindfold on Iola as Chet snapped pictures, when Joe tapped his shoulder again.

"Hey, do you hear that?" Joe asked.

"Hear what?" Frank replied.

"It sounds like there's someone outside the window!"

Frank tried to listen, but he couldn't hear anything over the music, the laughter of the kids, and the chatter of the parents in the next room. He moved closer to the window with Joe and looked out over the Zermeños' side yard. It was dark, so there wasn't much to see, and he didn't hear anything.

Frank shook his head. "I think you're hearing things, little brother."

But then he saw movement in the yard from the corner of his eye. It looked like someone running, but they disappeared from view too quickly for him to get a good look.

"Wait, I think you're right," Frank said. "I think someone *is* out there."

"Told ya!" Joe said.

"Come on," Frank said. "Let's go look out the front windows."

"Hey, where are you guys going?" Chet asked as they headed to the living room.

"We think there's someone outside," Joe said. "We're going to go check."

Speedy overheard them. "I'm coming too!"

The kids made their way to the windows at the front of the house. Chet had his camera pressed to his eye to take a picture and ended up stepping on the stuffed animal Tommy Dawson's little sister was playing with.

"You hurt Snuggles!" the girl shrieked.

"Sorry!" Chet said.

Frank crouched in front of one of the big windows next to the front door of the house, nothing but his eyes peeking over the windowsill. Joe stood next to him, peering around the edge of the curtains. Chet and Speedy took the window on the other side of the door.

"I can't see anything," Chet said. "It's too dark outside."

By now, the rest of the team had noticed them leaving the dining room and had gathered around them.

"What's going on?" Iola asked.

"We heard something weird outside," Joe replied.

"Speedy, do you have any lights out there?" Frank asked.

She nodded. "There's a porch light."

"Can you turn it on?" Frank said.

"You bet!" Speedy moved to a light switch on the wall near the door. "Count of three?"

Frank nodded.

"One . . . two . . ." Speedy flipped the switch. *"Three!"*

Outside on the Zermeños' lawn, three kids, all dressed in dark clothes, froze. Around them, the trees were covered in toilet paper, which hung from the branches like garlands and swayed gently in the breeze. The grass was covered in red and blue Silly String, which spelled out BANDITS STINK!

After a moment of stunned silence—the Bandits staring at the mess in the yard and the pranksters staring at them—everything exploded into action. The kids outside started to run, dropping their armfuls of extra toilet paper and Silly String bottles, and the Bandits poured out of the house after them.

Chapter

3

BANDITS VS. JUPITERS

"Stop them!" Frank yelled as the trio scattered in different directions. The Bandits took off after them. Frank and Joe ran toward Speedy's neighbors to the left, where the biggest of the pranksters had headed. Frank heard a cheer somewhere behind him as other members of the team caught one of the fleeing kids.

In the dark, Frank could just barely make out the outline of the person he was chasing. The kid ran around the side of the neighbor's house, and by the time Frank and Joe got there, he'd disappeared.

"Where did he go?" Joe said. "It's so dark out here."

"Shh," Frank whispered. "Let's just listen for a second."

The prankster couldn't have outrun them so fast. Frank was sure he was hiding somewhere among the bushes and trees in the yard. The two boys were silent for a moment, ears straining to pick up any sounds of movement, but they didn't hear anything.

Suddenly Frank had an idea.

"I guess we lost him," Frank said, loudly enough that his voice would carry across the yard. "Better just give up."

"What!" Joe squawked. "We can't just let him get away with—"

Frank nudged his brother and gave him a wink.

"There's no point, Joe," Frank said loudly. "Let's just go back."

Joe smiled as he understood his brother's plan. "Okay, you're right. Let's go."

The two boys walked away, pretending like they were headed back to Speedy's. But instead they hid around the corner of the neighbor's house. Frank held a finger to his lips, and Joe nodded. Now all they had to do was wait.

One minute passed, then two, and nothing happened. Frank began to think the prankster had actually gotten away. But then, just when he was about to give up, Frank heard the rustle of leaves as the other kid crept out of his hiding place behind a row of bushes.

"Go!" Frank cried.

He and Joe ran around the corner of the house. The prankster saw them and tried to get away, but Frank and Joe were too close. They caught the other kid, and all three of them went tumbling to the ground.

"We got 'im!" Joe exclaimed.

Frank looked into the prankster's face, which he could see for the first time.

"Conor Hound," he said. He should have known. Conor—a star player for the Bandits' rivals the

Jupiters—was the only boy he knew who was this big.

Coach Quinn came running around the corner, followed by a group of parents. "What's going on here?"

"We caught him, Coach Quinn!" Joe said. "This is one of the kids who was toilet-papering Speedy's house."

"You'd better come with me, Conor," the coach said. "Let him go, boys."

Frank, Joe, and Conor, who was hanging his head, followed Coach Quinn and the parents back to Speedy's house. Two other members of the Jupiters were already seated on the couch in the living room, their arms crossed over their chests. Conor sat down beside them with a scowl. Chet and Iola gave Frank and Joe high fives for catching him.

"I'm very disappointed by this unsportsmanlike behavior, gentlemen," Coach Quinn was saying to the Jupiters. "I'm going to have to call your parents."

"What a mess," Speedy said glumly, looking out the window at the toilet paper hanging from the trees.

"We'll help you clean it up," Iola promised.

"Yeah," Frank added. "Of course we will. Come on, everybody!"

"I think *they* should clean it up," Joe said, pointing at the boys on the couch.

"Yeah!" Speedy yelled. "They ruined our party. But I want to make sure we can see them clean up so they can't do anything else."

Mr. Zermeño held up his hand. "Why don't I grab some trash bags and everyone can help clean up the yard. I think Coach Quinn has some phone calls to make to these boys' parents."

The team collected empty trash bags from Mr. Zermeño and headed outside to take care of the mess the Jupiters had made. With so many people helping, it wouldn't take them long to clean up the yard. Frank and Joe picked Silly String up off the grass, while Tommy Dawson (the tallest member of the team) hoisted Iola (the shortest) onto his shoulders so she could reach the loops of toilet paper high in one of the trees. Speedy went back inside and grabbed a plate of cookies that everyone munched on as they worked.

"I'm going to take this bag inside and get another," Frank said when the trash bag he and Joe were sharing was stuffed with toilet paper and Silly String. "I'll be right back."

On his way to the kitchen for another trash bag, Frank passed Conor Hound and the other Jupiters. They were still sitting on the couch, waiting for Mr. Hound, who had agreed to take all three boys home. Coach Quinn was talking to them in her most disappointed voice. Frank actually felt kind of bad for them. If he knew anything about the coach of the Jupiters, Coach Riley, the joke would not be worth the extra minutes of running that the team would have to do at their next practice!

The player closest to Frank gave him a glare. "You'll be sorry," he said under his breath.

Well, maybe Frank didn't feel *that* bad for them.

With his head turned to look at Conor and the

others, Frank didn't notice Mimi lying on her stomach in his path until he'd tripped over her. She and the other younger kids were still spread out all over the living room floor, playing with the toys from Mimi's new backpack. The toys had invaded every surface, from the carpet to the coffee table.

"Hey!" Mimi squealed.

"Sorry!" Frank replied. He lifted his foot off her coloring book, which he'd accidentally stepped on. "I didn't see you."

Mrs. Morton poked her head around the corner. "Mimi, what did I say about getting in the way? Frank's the fourth person who's tripped over you tonight. How about you kids move into one of the bedrooms?"

"Mom!" Mimi protested. "Do we have to?"

While Mimi argued with her mother, Frank went into the kitchen to drop off his full garbage bag and pick up an empty one.

When he returned to the living room, Mimi and the younger kids were packing up her toys to move into one of the bedrooms, and Conor Hound's father had arrived. He'd already sent Conor and the other two players outside and was apologizing to Coach Quinn.

"I'm going to have a long talk with him tonight," he said.

"Smile!"

Frank was suddenly blinded by the flash of Chet's camera. He hadn't seen his friend approach, and now he couldn't see anything at all! He blinked to try to clear the bright dots from his vision.

"Hey, sorry!" Chet said. "I didn't mean to surprise you."

"Oh, that's okay," Frank said. "Can you help me back outside, though? I don't think I can make it on my own!"

Chet laughed and took Frank's arm. "Sure."

"Excuse me!" Mimi said.

The boys moved aside to let her pass. She had two stuffed animals cradled in her arms and more nearly spilling out of her partially unzipped backpack. She led the other younger brothers and sisters to one of the bedrooms so that no one else would trip over them.

Frank and Chet joined the rest of the Bandits outside, and soon they had finished cleaning the Zermeños' yard. Coach Quinn told them how proud she was of their teamwork as they came back inside the house and took the pieces of cake that Mrs. Zermeño had waiting for them. Then they all gathered together so that Chet could snap a team photo. After thanking the Zermeños for the party, everyone said good-bye and headed home.

PLAYBOOK PUZZLER

The next afternoon was their first official practice of the new season. The team was brimming with excitement as they gathered in the dugout at the Little League field. Frank took a deep breath, inhaling the smell of fresh grass and leather. As far as he was concerned, baseball season was the best time of the year.

Coach Quinn stood up in front of the team, her ever-present clipboard held in the crook of her arm, and everyone quieted down to listen to her instructions.

"I'm afraid I have some bad news, team," she said.

Frank exchanged a worried look with his brother.

"Remember the new playbook I showed you last night?" the coach said. "It's gone missing."

The team gasped.

"It went missing sometime during the party," Coach Quinn said. "Did any of you accidentally take it home with you?"

Frank looked at his teammates, but everyone was shaking their heads.

Coach Quinn sighed. She looked disappointed. "Well, I want you to check when you get home just in case, okay? That playbook is very important."

Frank swallowed. As far as he knew, he'd been the last one to look at the playbook.

"Okay, everyone," Coach Quinn said. "Time to get to work! Please break into pairs and do some catching and throwing."

Frank ran up to the coach as everyone else took the field to start practicing.

"Hey, Coach," he said. "I'm really sorry about the playbook."

"Thank you, Frank," she said.

"I put it on the coffee table in the living room when I was finished looking through it," Frank said. "Do you know if anyone else looked at it after I did?"

She shook her head. "I'm not sure. All I know is it was gone by the time I was ready to leave the Zermeños'. Don't worry, though. I'm sure it'll turn up."

Frank nodded and went to join Joe on the field. They began to toss a ball back and forth, listening to Coach Quinn's instructions about the best form to use as she weaved among the players, checking their progress.

When Coach Quinn was out of earshot, Joe said quietly to Frank, "I bet the playbook was stolen."

Frank shook his head. "Someone probably just took it by mistake."

"Oh, really?" Joe said. "What about what you told me that Jupiter said to you? 'You'll be sorry'? What better way to get back at us for getting them in trouble than by stealing our playbook?"

Frank thought about that. The boys' father, Fenton Hardy, was a private investigator, and he'd taught them how to look at the world through a PI's eyes. Frank thought back to the party and realized that the Jupiters players had been seated on the couch right next to the coffee table where he'd left the playbook. It would have been easy for one of them to swipe it when no one was looking, and Joe was right about one thing. It *would* be the perfect revenge.

"I guess it is possible," he said.

"Yes!" Joe said. "A new case for us to solve!"

Like their father, the boys had discovered they had a knack for solving mysteries. They'd already cracked several cases in Bayport and were always on the lookout for another. Frank wasn't convinced that this was a real mystery yet, but he decided to humor his brother just in case.

After practice was over, they returned home. But instead of going inside the house, they went to the woods out back where their father had built them a hidden tree house. They used it as their secret base of operations for all their investigations. Unless you knew what to look for, the tree house was perfectly hidden. Frank checked both ways to make sure no one was coming and then grabbed the rope they'd concealed behind a tree. When he gave it a tug, a rope ladder dropped down from the hidden tree house above. They climbed it quickly.

"Okay," Frank said once they were inside the tree house. He opened up the notebook where they kept track of clues for their investigations. "Let's start with the Five *W*s."

The Five *W*s was something else their father had taught them about investigations. Finding them was the key to solving any mystery. Frank took out his notebook and wrote them down.

"We don't know the *who*," Joe said, "but the *what* is the Bandits' playbook."

"*When* is sometime between when I looked at it after the team meeting and when Coach Quinn got ready to leave and noticed it was missing," Frank said. As he spoke, he filled in the answers in the notebook in his neat, straight handwriting. That was one reason he always took control of writing down the clues. Joe couldn't even read his own handwriting half the time.

"We should talk to everyone else who was at the party and see if anyone looked at it after you did," Joe pointed out. Frank made a note of it on the right side of the page, next to the Five Ws.

Who was the last person at the party to see the playbook?

"The *where* is the Zermeños' living room," Joe said, "and the *who* and *why* are what we have to figure out!"

A FURRY FRIEND

The boys joined the rest of the team on the field the next day for practice. Coach Quinn started the day off by asking them all a question.

"Did everyone check their things for the play-book yesterday?" she said.

The team nodded.

"Did anyone find it?" she asked.

Frank figured someone would say they had. It was a more likely explanation than the playbook having been stolen. But to his surprise, everyone shook their heads.

"I knew it!" Joe whispered. "It *was* stolen!"

"I guess you're right," Frank whispered back.

"That thief better watch out!" Joe said. "The Hardy brothers are on the case!"

The team took their positions to practice—which meant Frank behind home plate to catch and Joe at second base—so Frank didn't have a chance to talk to his brother about the playbook again until they were packing up their things to head home.

"Who do you think might have taken it?" Frank asked as he stuffed his mitt into his bag.

"That's easy!" Joe said. "We're still missing a *why*, right? That will lead us to our *who*! The thief has to be a person who had a *reason* to do it."

"A motive," Frank said. He and his brother started to walk across the park toward their house. "Either the thief wanted our playbook for themselves—"

"Or they just didn't want us to have it, " Joe said. "Neither motive fits for anyone on the Bandits."

"But *both* fit for the Jupiters players," Frank

pointed out. "Stealing our playbook is a great way to get back at us for getting them into trouble."

"Plus," Joe added, "it would give their team an advantage to know about all the special training ideas and plays that Coach Quinn put together."

"You're right," Frank said. "The Jupiters had the perfect motive."

Joe looked over at another team practicing at one of the other baseball diamonds at the park. "Hey, is that the Jupiters?"

Frank followed his brother's gaze. "Yeah, I think it is."

"Let's go over there," Joe said. "Maybe we'll discover something!"

Frank followed his brother to the field where the other team was practicing. Sure enough, it was the Jupiters. Frank would recognize Conor Hound anywhere, since he towered almost a foot above all the other kids on the team. Frank and Joe crept toward the dugout as the team practiced catching and throwing the way the Bandits had done the day before. As long as they stayed low to the ground, the team wouldn't be able to spot them over the roof of the dugout, which stuck up several feet out of the ground.

"Well, now what?" Frank whispered once they were crouched behind the dugout.

Joe shrugged. "We wait? Maybe when they come back here to pick up their stuff after practice, they'll talk about stealing the playbook."

"Maybe," Frank said. "What would really be good is if we could get into the dugout and see if the playbook is in there. If one of them stole it, they probably would have brought it here with them."

"Yeah, but how do we get in there without anyone noticing?" Joe asked.

"Uh, I'm still working on that part of the plan," Frank replied.

Joe sighed. "Well, let me know when you figure it out."

They watched the Jupiters practicing for a couple of minutes, Frank racking his brain for a plan. Suddenly there was a commotion in the far corner of the field. Frank shielded his eyes from the sun with one hand as he tried to see what was going on. Two players were running toward the back of the field and shouting, and in the distance Frank spotted Wilmer Mack. Mr. Mack often brought his dog, Lucy, out to the ball field for her daily walk, and Lucy loved playing fetch more than anything.

"Hey, look!" Joe said, pointing. "It's Lucy! She has their ball!"

Sure enough, there was Lucy with a baseball in her mouth. The two Jupiters players who had been tossing it back and forth were running after her, trying to get their ball back. But Lucy just thought it was part of the game. She dodged away from them, leading them on a chase across the field. Slowly, more and more Jupiters players went to help until finally the whole team, Coach Riley, and Mr. Mack were chasing Lucy, who was having the time of her life.

"Now's our chance!" Joe cried, jumping to his feet and rushing into the dugout.

"Joe!" Frank said. "Get back here!"

But Joe was already looking through the dugout

for the bright-red playbook. First he went through the coach's papers, which were stacked on the edge of the bench. Then he grabbed Conor Hound's backpack—which had his last name monogrammed on it in big letters—and began to look through that, too.

"They're going to catch you!" Frank warned.

"No way," Joe replied. "It will take them forever to catch Lucy. But if you come down here and help me, we'll be done twice as fast!"

Frank looked nervously out at the field. The team was still chasing Lucy, and they were now entirely off the field and halfway to the concessions stand. Someone could come back any second, but for now, the Jupiters were completely distracted.

"Oh man," Frank said, looking back and forth between his brother in the dugout and the Jupiters chasing the dog. "Fine! I'm coming!"

Frank jumped down into the dugout with Joe and started looking through the backpacks and gym bags the team had left scattered around. He felt a little bad about it, but he reassured himself that he wasn't hurting anything. Plus, the Jupiters had started it by vandalizing Speedy's yard and stealing the playbook in the first place.

"See anything?" Joe asked.

Frank shook his head. "Just equipment, clothes, and homework."

"Same here," Joe said.

Frank looked back over the field. The team had finally caught Lucy, and Mr. Mack was getting the ball back from her.

"We've got to go," Frank said. "They'll be headed back soon."

"Okay," Joe said. "There's nothing here anyway. Let's go!"

The two boys climbed out of the dugout and began to run back toward their house, in the opposite direction, just as the Jupiters started to return to the field to resume their practice.

"Maybe the Jupiters players weren't the ones who took the playbook after all," Frank said.

"Just because we didn't find the playbook doesn't mean they don't have it," Joe pointed out. "If it wasn't them, then who was it?"

PHOTOGRAPHIC EVIDENCE

Frank and Joe returned home and had dinner with their parents and Aunt Trudy. Frank had trouble concentrating on his mother's story about what had happened at her job that day and Aunt Trudy's story about the book she was reading, because he couldn't stop thinking about the missing playbook. The Jupiters were the only people at Speedy's house that night who had any motive to steal it. Plus, they had been alone in the living room with the book more than anyone else, which gave them plenty of time to swipe it. He thought about it as they ate dessert, as they cleaned the table, and as he started to wash the dishes (it was his turn). If the Jupiters had stolen the playbook, wouldn't they have wanted to show it to their teammates and brag about what they'd done? Frank thought so. In that case, he and Joe should have found it in the dugout.

"Frank?" Mrs. Hardy called, shaking him from his thoughts.

"Yeah, Mom?" he said.

She held the phone out to him. "It's for you."

He wiped his hands dry on a dish towel and took the phone. "Hello?"

"Hey, Frank!" It was Chet on the other end of the line. "Do you and Joe want to come over and play video games tonight? My parents said it's okay."

Chet! Frank suddenly remembered that Chet had been snapping photos throughout the party. Maybe somewhere in his pictures he'd captured a clue as to who had taken the playbook.

Frank turned to his mother, who was drying the dishes he'd washed.

"Hey, Mom, is it okay if we go over to Chet's for a little while tonight?" he asked.

Mrs. Hardy gave him a look.

"Once I'm done with the dishes, of course," he added with an extra-sweet smile.

"I don't know, Frank . . . ," she said.

"Please, Mom!" Frank pleaded. He *had* to see those photos. Chet might have even photographed the theft itself!

"Is your homework done?" Mrs. Hardy asked.

Frank nodded. "Totally done. My chores, too."

Mrs. Hardy thought for a moment. Frank crossed his fingers and, for good measure, tried to cross his toes as well.

"All right," she finally said. "Just be home by eight, okay? It's a school night."

"I will," Frank promised. "Thanks, Mom!"

"Finish the dishes first!" Mrs. Hardy pointed to the sink.

Frank nodded and got back to scrubbing.

A few minutes later Frank and Joe walked over to the Mortons' house. On the way, Frank told Joe about his theory that there might be clues hidden in Chet's photographs from the party.

"Thank goodness for Chet's new hobby!" Joe said, and Frank laughed.

When they arrived, Chet answered the door and invited them into the house.

"I just got this new race-car game, Ultimate Driver," Chet told them as they went into the living room. "It's so cool. You're going to love it!"

"Not yet, Chet!" Iola said. She and Mimi were sitting on the carpet in front of the television, watching an animated movie about a horse. "Mom said you have to let us finish our movie before you can play."

"Yeah, sorry about that," Chet said to Frank and Joe. "They got here first, so we have to wait."

"That's okay," Frank said. "We were actually wondering if we could look at your pictures from the party."

"Sure!" Chet said. "I think they turned out pretty well. They're on my dad's computer. Follow me."

Chet led them upstairs, to a spare bedroom that Mr. Morton used as his home office. Chet sat down in front of the computer and jiggled the mouse to wake it up while Frank and Joe pulled up chairs. Chet opened up a folder, and a file with dozens and dozens of pictures in it came up. Frank exchanged a look with his brother. Going through Chet's pictures to look for clues was going to take a lot longer than he'd thought!

Chet started to click through the pictures. They started at the beginning of the evening, when everyone was in the Zermeños' backyard, eating and playing games. Joe asked Chet if he could skip ahead.

"What are you looking for?" Chet asked.

"Well, we want to see if there are any clues about who took the playbook Coach Quinn showed us that night," Frank said.

"Someone stole it?" Chet asked.

Of course, Frank realized. Chet wasn't on the team, so he didn't know that the playbook had gone missing. Frank explained to him that the playbook had disappeared at some point during the party.

"So you two are on the case, huh?" Chet asked.

Joe grinned. "Of course we are!"

"Well, let's see if I can help," Chet said. He clicked quickly through the pictures until he came to one of Coach Quinn standing in front of the team in the Zermeños' living room, holding the playbook in her hands. "I took this during the team meeting. This was the first time you saw the playbook, right?"

Frank nodded. "Yeah. Keep going, Chet."

Chet clicked slowly through the pictures. There were a couple more of the team meeting, then one of Ezra Moore and Tommy Dawson high-fiving.

In the background, Frank was looking through the playbook. In the next picture, Speedy was laughing with first baseman Jason Prime. Frank had disappeared from the background, and the playbook was sitting on the coffee table where he'd left it.

"Well, it looks like it wasn't *you* who stole it, Frank," Joe said.

Frank punched him in the arm while Chet laughed.

After that, the pictures moved outside. There were at least a dozen showing members of the team working together to clean up the Zermeños' yard.

"You can skip these," Joe said. "Did you take any more in the living room?"

"Sure did," Chet replied. He clicked forward until the pictures moved from the Zermeños' dark yard to their bright living room. There was one of several parents in the kitchen, smiling and waving at the camera. Then there was a picture of Frank looking shocked. Frank remembered he was holding a trash bag at that moment. He hadn't seen Chet there, and the flash of the camera had temporarily blinded him. Joe laughed at the goofy expression on Frank's face in the picture, but Frank studied the photo with sharp eyes.

"There!" Frank said. In the bottom corner of the picture was a splotch of red on top of the coffee table. It was a little fuzzy, but Joe had a feeling he knew what that red splotch was.

Joe put his face close to the computer and squinted at the picture. "Yeah, that's definitely the playbook."

Frank frowned and crossed his arms over his chest.

"What's wrong?" Chet asked.

Frank sighed. "The Jupiters didn't steal the play-book."

Chapter 7

BANDIT BETRAYAL

"What?" Joe said. "How do you know?"

"Because the Jupiters were gone by that point," Frank said. "When I came out of the kitchen with the empty trash bag, Conor Hound's dad had already arrived and sent them outside to wait for him."

"Are you sure?" Joe said. "Maybe Mr. Hound didn't arrive until later."

"I'm positive," Frank said. "That was the only time I went inside while we were cleaning the yard."

"You know what, I think you're right," Joe said. "When you went inside, I went over to help Speedy instead. I remember she and I were trying to get some toilet paper out of a tree with a rake when we saw the Jupiters getting into Mr. Hound's car."

"But the playbook was still on the coffee table right where I left it," Frank said, pointing to the red splotch in the picture. "The Jupiters couldn't have stolen it. Which means . . ."

"What?" Chet asked.

"It means it was one of *us* who stole it," Frank said slowly. "One of the Bandits."

"Oh man," Joe said, leaning back in his chair with a frown.

All three boys just looked at one another for a moment. Frank's stomach suddenly ached. He didn't *want* to solve this mystery anymore. Not if the thief was someone on his own team.

"Keep going, Chet," Joe finally said. "Maybe there are more clues to find."

Chet continued to click through the pictures, but neither the coffee table nor the playbook could be seen in any of them. Until he reached the last picture. It was the photograph he'd taken of most of the team at the end of the night. They all had their arms around one another, big grins on their faces.

On the coffee table in front of them, the playbook was nowhere in sight.

Frank and Joe decided to forget about the case for the rest of the night. It made them both too sad to imagine that one of the Bandits had stolen the playbook. Instead they played video games with Chet and tried not to think about it.

By the next morning, though, Frank was once again determined to find out who was behind the playbook's disappearance. The thief might be someone he liked, but he still had to get to the bottom of the mystery. He owed that to Coach Quinn and the rest of the team. Joe told him at breakfast that he'd woken up feeling the same way.

"The thing I don't get," Joe said over pancakes at the kitchen table, "is why any of the Bandits would have a *motive* to steal the playbook. It hurts the team, and whoever they are, they're on the team! It doesn't make any sense."

Frank had been thinking about the same thing. Why would a Bandit want to hurt the Bandits?

"I don't understand it either," he said. "Do you remember anyone acting strangely that night?"

Joe shrugged. "Not really. Oh! Except Tommy Dawson. He was in a really bad mood, remember?"

"Oh yeah!" Frank said. "He was upset about not getting to pitch."

"Right!" Joe exclaimed. "He was supposed to pitch in Speedy's place because of her hurt wrist. But

⇆ 127

when Speedy got better, Coach Quinn told him she was going to start Speedy instead."

"He was pretty angry about that," Frank remembered. "Maybe angry enough to want to get revenge on Coach Quinn . . ."

"By stealing the playbook she made," Joe finished. "Would Tommy have had a chance to do it? The team was together most of the night. When would he have taken it?"

Frank thought back to the night of the party. The playbook went missing sometime between when the Jupiters left and when Chet took the group photo at the end of the night. For most of that time, the team was outside cleaning up the Zermeños' yard, but kids did come and go from the yard the whole time they were out there.

"He might have had a chance," Frank said, "if he went inside while the rest of us were in the yard. The younger kids were playing in Speedy's bedroom by then, and most of the parents were in the kitchen. There wouldn't have been anyone in the living room to see him swipe the playbook."

"But did he go inside while we were in the yard?" Joe asked.

"Only one way to find out," Frank said. "Hurry and finish your breakfast quick. We've got to stop by the Mortons' before school!"

Joe wolfed down the rest of his pancakes, and he and Frank left for school. They usually walked anyway, so today they made a detour to Chet's house on the way.

"Hey, guys!" Chet said when he answered the door. He looked happy to see them but puzzled. "What are you doing here?"

"Can we look at those pictures again, Chet?" Frank asked.

Chet checked his watch. "I think we've got time if we hurry! What are you looking for?"

The three boys ran upstairs to Mr. Morton's office while Frank explained their new theory. Chet fired up the computer and found the pictures he'd taken of the team outside cleaning, the same ones they had skipped the night before. They went through them slowly, scouring the pictures for clues, their faces just inches from the computer screen.

"There!" Joe said.

The photograph was of Speedy holding an armful of toilet paper. In the background was the front door of her house. It was partially open, spilling light across the lawn. Tommy Dawson was stepping inside.

"He *did* go inside while we were working," Frank said, "which means he would have had the chance to take the playbook."

Joe nodded. "I guess it's time to talk to Tommy. Let's get to school!"

PITCH WARS

"You ready?" Frank asked his brother when they spotted Tommy Dawson near the gym after school. They'd been keeping an eye on Tommy's gym locker ever since the bell rang. They had baseball practice right after school, so they knew Tommy would eventually go to his locker to pick up his gym bag.

"I'm ready," Joe said. "Let's do this."

Joe approached Tommy as he reached his locker

and started to spin the combination lock. Frank waited farther down the hall. Tommy looked up when Joe approached.

"Hi, Joe," he said. "How's it going?"

"Pretty good," Joe replied. Then he launched into the conversation he and Frank had rehearsed. "I just wanted to say, I'm really sorry you're not going to be pitching in the first game."

"Thanks," Tommy said, putting his math book down and grabbing some stuff from his locker. Joe moved to the other side of the locker, so that Tommy would have to turn his back to his open locker to face him.

"The truth is," Joe continued, "I think you're a better pitcher than Speedy any day."

"You and me both," Tommy said, getting annoyed. "It's so unfair! Coach Quinn told me *I* was going to get to pitch in the first game. Just because Speedy got better faster than anyone expected shouldn't change anything."

With Tommy's back turned to him while he was complaining to Joe, Frank crept toward Tommy's open locker. If Tommy had stolen the playbook, the odds were high that this was where he was keeping it. A private place with a lock on it.

"Yeah, that's really uncool," Joe said.

Tommy crossed his arms over his chest. "I bet Coach Quinn just wants to put Speedy in because she's a girl like the coach. I can't believe a *girl* is getting to pitch over me."

Frank rolled his eyes behind Tommy's back. Speedy was the best pitcher in the league. It had nothing to do with her being a girl. Frank quietly inched Tommy's locker door open enough that he could peer inside.

"This whole thing makes me so mad," Joe said. "It almost . . ."

"What?" Tommy asked.

"Well . . . ," Joe said. Frank had never realized just how good an actor his brother was. He really seemed upset on Tommy's behalf. "It almost makes me want to get back at the coach somehow, you know?"

Tommy's locker was a mess of papers, books, broken pencils, and dirty clothes. Frank didn't see the playbook, but it could easily be buried under all the junk crammed inside. Frank reached inside and began to move things around, moving slowly and carefully so as not to make any noise.

Meanwhile, Tommy didn't take the bait Joe had laid out for him. Instead he just shrugged and said, "It's not *that* big a deal. It just made me mad, you know?"

"Yeah, I get it," Joe said, "but are you sure you want to let Coach Quinn off the hook that easy?"

Tommy looked at Joe with sudden suspicion in his face. "What are you trying to say?" he asked.

Uh-oh. Frank knew he had to move fast. He moved a couple of Tommy's textbooks and looked underneath a dirty (and kind of smelly) T-shirt. He still didn't see the playbook, but that didn't mean it wasn't still buried in there somewhere. . . .

Joe said, "I'm not saying anything, Tommy."

"Are you trying to ask me if *I'm* the one who took the playbook?" Tommy asked. "To get back at Coach Quinn for letting Speedy pitch instead of me?"

"No!" Joe said. "I just—"

Tommy started to turn back to his locker. Frank saw the movement from the corner of his eye as he rooted around for the playbook, but it was too late. Tommy was going to catch him in the act.

"No way, man!" Joe exclaimed, grabbing Tommy's shoulders so he couldn't turn. "I would never think that, Tommy!"

Frank snatched his hand back from the locker

and leaned against the wall as he tried to catch his breath. He didn't know how real private investigators like his dad handled all this excitement!

Joe found him there a minute later after saying good-bye to Tommy.

"Did you find anything?" Joe asked.

Frank shook his head. "The playbook might have been in there, if he buried it at the bottom of the mess, but I didn't see it."

"I don't know about this, Frank," Joe said. "Tommy seemed really upset at me for thinking he'd taken the playbook. It didn't seem like an act."

"I know what you mean," Frank said, "but right now, we don't have any other suspects. Tommy had the opportunity to take it *and* a motive. He's the only one we can think of with any reason to want the playbook to disappear."

Joe frowned. "We've got to be missing something."

"I agree," Frank said. "But what?"

HIDING SPOT

Frank and Joe decided to take a break from the
case for the rest of the day. They were a little
stumped and didn't know what to do next. Their
dad always said that sometimes the best thing you
could do was to think about something else for
a while instead. After baseball practice—which
Chet attended to get some pictures of the team in
action—Frank asked him if they could hang out
that afternoon.

"That would be great!" Chet said. "Want to come to my house? We can play Ultimate Driver again."

"Sounds good!" Frank and Joe said.

The three boys went over to Chet's house, and Frank called his mom to let her know where they were before they sat in the living room to play Chet's new racing game. Chet wasn't very good at sports like Frank and Joe, but he was awesome at video games. In fact, he was crushing them. His red car zoomed ahead of their green and blue ones, tearing around corners and flying over obstacles. At one point Iola came into the living room to watch.

"Come on, Frank!" she cheered. She always rooted for the underdog, and Frank's green car was at the back of the pack. "You can do it!"

"Hey!" Joe complained. "What about me?"

"Or me?" Chet asked. "I'm your brother!"

"Sorry," Iola replied. "Frank needs my cheers the most!"

"Ha-ha, thanks a lot," Frank said, but he secretly appreciated her support.

Unfortunately, Iola's cheers couldn't make Frank's

car move faster. Chet's car raced across the finish line first, and Frank was a distant third.

"Yes!" Chet shouted, pumping his fist in the air. Frank and Joe both gave him high fives.

Mrs. Morton appeared in the doorway. "Anyone want a snack?"

"Yes, please!" everyone said.

Mrs. Morton brought them a plate of apple slices with peanut butter. Mimi, with her pink backpack on, followed her into the living room.

"Chet, Iola," Mrs. Morton said. "Can you keep an eye on your sister for a minute? Jeanine from next door is having some kind of baking emergency and needs my help."

"Sure thing, Mom," Chet said.

After they'd eaten the apple slices, Joe challenged Chet and Frank to an Ultimate Driver rematch. Iola decided she wanted to play too and chose a yellow car to drive. They offered to let Mimi join the game, but she wasn't interested. Instead she unzipped her backpack and turned it upside down. A small avalanche of toys, crayons, and coloring books came tumbling out of it. Mimi selected an orange crayon and began to color in a picture of a giraffe.

"I'm going to get you this time, Chet!" Joe said as the race began. Chet's red car zoomed into the lead, but halfway down the course, Joe took a tight turn on the racetrack that cut his lead in half. Joe was almost as good at video games as Chet was.

"Keep dreaming, Joe!" Chet teased. "You'll never beat me!"

Out of nowhere, Iola's yellow car passed everyone else.

"Take that, boys!" she said, laughing.

Meanwhile, Frank accidentally crashed his car into a tree and fell farther behind. "Oh man!" he said.

Joe, Chet, and Iola were locked in a fierce battle for first place. Frank was working hard to catch up, but he knew it was hopeless. The finish line approached, and Joe's car inched ahead. Frank could see that Joe was crossing his fingers, which made it hard for him to hold the controller.

"Come on!" Joe said, urging his car forward.

Joe's car raced across the finish line first, and he jumped up and did a victory dance. Frank and Chet groaned good-naturedly, while Iola laughed and threw a couch cushion at him.

"Good race, guys," Chet said.

"Thanks," Joe said. "Want to go again?"

"Yeah!" Iola said.

"I'm going to take a break this round," Frank said.

"What, are you chicken?" Chet teased.

Frank made a squawking sound, and everyone laughed. While they cued up the game, he sat next to Mimi on the carpet.

"Hey, Mimi," he said. "Have you started preschool yet?" He remembered that was why her parents had bought her the backpack in the first place. She'd been so excited to start school when he'd last seen her, at the Bandits' party.

Mimi nodded without looking up from her picture. "Yeah, I started this week."

The others had begun another race and were whooping, hollering, and teasing one another. Frank picked up a green crayon.

"Do you mind?" he asked, pointing to the tree the giraffe was eating from. It hadn't been colored in yet.

"Go ahead," Mimi said.

"So, are you liking school?" Frank asked as he started to color in the leaves of the tree.

"Yeah, it's pretty cool," Mimi said.

"Are you learning to read?" Frank asked.

"Not yet," she said, "but we're learning letters, and we play lots of games, and there's recess and snack, and my best friend Jill is in my class, and my teacher is really nice. . . ."

Mimi talked nonstop about school after that. She could give Speedy a run for her money when it came to words spoken per minute. Together she and Frank colored in the giraffe picture and another one that featured two lions drinking from a watering hole. Chet, Iola, and Joe were playing another round of Ultimate Driver when Mrs. Morton came home from the baking emergency next door.

"Mimi," she said, "it's almost time for ballet. Better start getting ready."

"Okay, Mom," Mimi said. She scooped up all the toys and crayons and shoved them into her backpack. Then she ran out of the room to get ready for her dance class.

Frank moved back to where the others sat in front of the television. They'd had enough of Ultimate Driver and were putting in a different video game. But something was bugging Frank as he tried to beat the evil lizard king in the new game. Something he couldn't put into words yet, something that had struck him when he'd seen Mimi picking up her toys earlier. . . .

"Earth to Frank!" Iola said. "Are you going to pick up that power crystal or just stare at it?"

Then, all of a sudden, it became clear. Frank dropped his controller.

"I know what happened to the playbook!" he exclaimed.

Can you solve the mystery? How did Frank figure out what happened?

And, most importantly, who took the Bandits' playbook?

THE HARDY BOYS—and
YOUR!

CAN YOU SOLVE THE MYSTERY OF THE MISSING PLAYBOOK?

Grab a piece of paper and write your answers down.
Or just turn the page to find out!

1. Frank and Joe came up with a list of suspects.
   Can you think of more? List your suspects.

2. Write down the way you think the brand-
   new Bayport Bandits' playbook disappeared.

3. Which clues helped you to solve this mystery?
   Write them down.

PLAY BALL!

"Wait, what?" Joe said, glancing at Frank as he dropped his controller too.

"I figured out who stole the playbook!" Frank repeated. "Well, not *stole* it exactly."

Iola paused the game. "Well? Tell us!"

"I can do better than that," Frank declared. "I can show you."

Frank ran up the stairs to the second floor of the Mortons' home, followed by Joe, Chet, and Iola.

He turned left at the top of the stairs and headed to Mimi's room, which had a pink and purple sign on the door bearing her name. Frank knocked, and Mimi—dressed in her ballet uniform—opened the door.

She cocked her head at them. "What do you want?"

"Can we come in for a second?" Frank asked.

She let them inside and Chet asked, "What's going on, Frank?"

"Mimi, do you remember what you were doing the night of the Bandits' party?" Frank asked.

The little girl nodded. "Me and the other little kids were playing."

"Where?" Frank asked.

"In the living room, mostly."

"On the floor," Frank said. "Just like you were downstairs just now, right?"

"Yeah," she said. "So?"

"So a lot of people tripped over you, didn't they?" he asked.

"I guess," she said. "*You* stepped on my coloring book."

"I sure did," Frank agreed. He turned to the

others. "It was right after I came inside to get a new trash bag. I tripped over Mimi, went into the kitchen for the bag, and when I came out, the Jupiters were gone. That's when you took that picture of me, Chet."

"The one that showed that the playbook was still on the coffee table," Chet said.

"Right," Frank said. "The playbook was still on the coffee table after I got the new trash bag, but sometime between then and the end of the night, it disappeared. Mimi, do you remember what happened after I tripped over you and stepped on your book?"

Mimi nodded. "Mom made me and the other kids move to Speedy's bedroom so we wouldn't be in the way."

"What did you have to do in order to move?" Frank asked.

"Put my toys and stuff into my backpack."

"Oh!" Joe said. "I get it! Mimi, where do you keep all your toys?"

Mimi pointed to a small chest underneath her window.

"Do you mind if we look in it?" Joe asked.

She shrugged. "I guess not."

Joe opened the chest, and he and Frank rifled through it. There were dozens of stuffed animals, building blocks, action figures, and coloring books. And then, near the bottom, sandwiched between two coloring books, was a bright-red notebook with PLAYBOOK written on the front in block letters. Frank held it up in triumph.

"You found it!" Iola shrieked. She gave Frank and Joe high fives.

Chet laughed. "So *Mimi* stole the playbook?"

Frank smiled. "Not on purpose. Mimi can't read

yet. When her mom told her to pack her things and move to the bedroom, she accidentally grabbed it along with her coloring books."

"Oops!" Mimi said, giggling. "Sorry!"

Everyone laughed, and Chet gave his youngest sister a hug and assured her it was okay.

"Case closed!" Frank said.

Well, not quite. First they had to return the playbook. At baseball practice the next day, Coach Quinn started with her usual pep talk and instructions. Before she could finish, though, Frank raised his hand.

"Yes, Frank?" the coach asked.

"I was just wondering," Frank said, reaching into his bag, "if you were still looking for this?"

He showed her the playbook, and the team erupted into applause. Coach Quinn took the playbook back with a big smile.

"Good work, Frank!" she said happily. "You found it!"

"With Joe and Chet's help," Frank said.

"Well, in that case," Coach Quinn said, "I think

I'll have to treat my whole team—and the team's official photographer—to ice cream cones after practice!"

The team cheered, and Chet snapped a picture.

"Okay, everyone!" Coach Quinn clapped her hands. "Let's get to work!"

As everyone was moving to their positions to start practice, Frank and Joe caught up to Tommy Dawson.

"Hey, Tommy," Joe said. "I'm sorry I accused you of stealing the playbook with no proof."

Tommy sighed. "It's okay. I was being a real jerk about Speedy. I would have suspected me too."

"So, friends?" Joe asked.

Tommy grinned. "You bet."

After baseball practice, Frank and Joe went into the woods behind their house and climbed the rope ladder to their hidden tree house. Joe took out their notebook and a pen.

"I'm glad Tommy wasn't the person who took it," Frank said.

"Me too," said Joe. "And I am really happy we cracked this case!"

WATER-SKI WIPEOUT

A CABIN IN THE WOODS

As the tour bus pulled up outside the lodge, Frank and Joe Hardy could see the lake in the distance. Bucks Mountain, the tallest peak near their hometown, Bayport, was right behind it.

"You think we could hike all the way to the top?" Frank asked, turning to his younger brother.

"It's probably too steep," eight-year-old Joe replied. "Besides, don't you want to spend all day out on the boat? That's why I brought the skis."

Nine-year-old Frank looked at the luggage rack above them. His brother's new water skis were tied together on the luggage rack with a bright blue strap. Last summer Joe had started water-skiing at camp. In just a few weeks, he'd gotten really good. He even tried to ski for a few seconds on just one ski—even though he usually ended up in the water! Joe was so excited about waterskiing, this year their parents had bought him his very own set of skis for Christmas. And he was ready to break them in at the third and fourth graders' school trip to Lake Poketoe. This would be the very first time he used them.

"You'll have to teach me," Frank said. "I doubt I'll be as good as you."

Ellie Freeman's head popped up over the seat in front of them. She was wearing her Bayport Bandits T-shirt. She was on their baseball team, and she liked wearing the uniform even when she didn't have to. "You promised to teach me too," she said, looking at Joe. "I want to learn how to do a flip!"

Joe laughed. "Like the professionals do? That's really hard. I don't think I'm going to be able to do that for a while!"

Ellie hopped out of her seat and grabbed her duffel bag from the rack above. "I guess I can try. . . . Are you guys going to the barbecue tonight?"

"You bet," Joe said. "Mr. Morton promised he'd make his famous smoked ribs." Mr. Morton, their good friend Chet's dad, was one of the parents who had come along on the school trip. Suzie Klein's mother had also come, but as far as Joe knew, she didn't make ribs as good as Mr. Morton's.

Joe reached for the water skis on the rack above, and they came down with a clatter as he tried to take them down.

"Ow! Watch it, Hardys."

Frank and Joe turned around to see Adam Ackerman in the seat behind them. Adam was in Frank's grade at school. He was sitting with his friend Paul. Adam was on the aisle, and he kept rubbing the side of his head.

"You hit me with those stupid skis!" Adam

complained. He stood up, yanking his bag down from the rack above. "You're going to pay for that, Hardy."

He pushed past them, nearly knocking Joe over. Paul followed close behind. He was a short boy with a large, round face. He always wore his brown baseball cap turned to the side. "Watch your back, Hardy," he grumbled.

"Just ignore them," Frank said. "It's not worth it."

But Joe's cheeks were hot. He felt like everyone on the bus was staring at him. "Let's go," he said, careful not to knock anyone else with the skis.

Adam was one of the biggest bullies at Bayport Elementary. He was taller than most of the kids and was always saying mean things or pushing people around. Frank and Joe tried to stay away from him, but even they had trouble with him sometimes.

The Hardys followed Ellie out of the bus, looking at the lake in front of them. A few kids had dropped their bags on the rocky beach. They crowded around Mrs. Jones, one of the parents who had come on the trip. She gave them directions as to which cabins were theirs. Frank and Joe found out they'd be staying in the lodge itself.

Just hearing the birds chirping put Joe in a better mood. The afternoon sun was out and the water looked cool and refreshing. A few yards away, a boat was zipping across the lake. A girl was in an inner tube behind it, screaming as it pulled her along.

"Frank and Joe Hardy! What a pleasant surprise!" Mrs. Rodriguez called out from the lodge. She'd been Joe's second-grade teacher, and she was one of the adults who'd come on the other bus. It was funny to see her in plaid shorts and a pink T-shirt. Joe hadn't ever seen her outside the classroom!

"This is the best!" Joe called out. "Glad we caught the last few hours of sunshine."

"It's good to have you here, just in case. . . . You never know what might happen!" Mrs. Rodriguez smiled. Just a few months ago Joe and Frank had helped her find a ring that she'd lost. She'd thought someone at school had stolen it, but the boys figured out that wasn't true. They eventually found it in one of her desk drawers.

It wasn't the first case they'd solved, though. Frank and Joe were known around Bayport for solving mysteries. Once it was a lost video game and another time it was a missing playbook. Their father, Fenton Hardy, was a private detective. He'd taught them everything they knew about investigating. He showed them how to interview suspects and search a crime scene for clues.

Joe dragged his water skis behind him. He was happy the path to the lodge wasn't that long—the skis were getting heavy! They followed the rest of their group into the lodge. There was a huge living room with couches. A few deer heads were on the wall above the fireplace.

"Whoa," Frank whispered. "That's kind of creepy."

"It's like a real log cabin," Joe said. He pointed to the ceiling, where you could see all the wood beams. It reminded him of the toys he and Frank played with when they were really little.

Frank looked out the back windows, toward the lake. There were a few small cabins there, hidden in the trees. He saw Adam and Paul go into one of them with their bags. A sign in the ground near the front said PINECONE CABIN.

Just then Chet Morton came down the hallway. "Did you guys pick your bunks yet?" he asked. "You should come check out our room! We left you a top and bottom bunk!"

They followed him down the hall, to a room with two sets of bunk beds. Mr. Morton was sitting on one. He pulled a jar of red stuff from his bag. "My secret rib sauce!" He smiled. "I'll need this for tonight."

Frank and Joe laughed. "I call dibs on the top bunk!" Joe declared. He looked around, realizing there wasn't a good place to leave his skis. "Where should I put these?" he asked. "They take up the whole room."

"There's a shed out back," Chet said. "Here, I'll show you."

As Chet ran out the door, his dad called after him. "You can go explore, but make sure you're back in an hour. Dinner will be served!"

Chet showed Frank and Joe the storage shed behind the lodge. There were a dozen other cabins around it. Joe put his skis inside, next to a pile of life vests. Then the boys followed Chet down to the dock.

"Wow, there are kayaks!" Frank said.

"And we can use that tomorrow morning," Chet added, pointing to a white speedboat tied to the dock. "Joe, remember, you promised me you'd teach me to water ski!"

"He promised you . . . and me . . . and Ellie . . . and half the school," Frank laughed. "It's going to be a long day."

Joe smiled as they walked back to the lodge. A crowd had gathered on the deck. Mr. Morton, Mrs. Rodriguez, and some of the other adults were cooking dinner. Some kids were sitting at the round tables, drinking lemonade. Ellie and a few of her friends were tossing a softball back and forth on the grass below.

As the sun set, Joe could almost picture what it would be like tomorrow. All his friends would be out on the boat. He'd teach them how to do different tricks on his water skis. Maybe they'd even go tubing afterward.

"Who's ready to eat?" Mr. Morton called out. A bunch of kids cheered.

Joe, Frank, and Chet all cheered along with them. One thing was certain: this was going to be the best school trip yet.

CHOOSE YOUR OWN ADVENTURE

"Today we'll have three groups heading out," Mr. Morton told everyone the next morning when they'd gathered at picnic tables outside the lodge for breakfast. "Mrs. Rodriguez will be taking a group to the other side of the lake, to hike Bucks Mountain. You'll learn about all the wildlife in this region and collect samples of leaves from trees native to this forest. All of you have to go at some point, either today or tomorrow."

166 ⇄

"Awesome!" Billy Krueger called out. He was in the same class as Frank and always seemed to have a smile on his face. "I want to see a bear! I'm in!"

Mr. Morton laughed. "Wait one minute—I'm not done yet. Mrs. Pinkelton will be doing nature crafts in the lodge this morning, and I'll take a group out on the boat. She'll be doing fish, leaf, and flower prints. I'll take you tubing and skiing, yes, but then I'll take you guys past Seaway Island, home to Native American artifacts. After lunch, we'll switch groups so everyone gets to do two different activities today."

Ellie Freeman raised her hand and called out, "Is Joe Hardy going out on the boat this morning?"

Mr. Morton pointed to Joe, who was sitting at one of the tables, eating breakfast with Frank and Chet. "You'll have to ask him." Then he went inside the lodge.

Joe had a forkful of eggs in his mouth. Before he could even look up, Ellie and four of her friends were around the table. Two of the girls were on the Bayport club soccer team. Joe recognized their blue-and-white T-shirts. "Can we borrow your water skis too?" a girl with blond pigtails asked.

Joe swallowed his bite. "Sure."

"Our friends Jack and Connor want to come out on the boat, but only if they can water-ski too. Is that okay?" a girl with freckles asked.

Frank smiled. "Everyone can come. Joe will give waterskiing lessons to everyone!"

Ellie and her friends seemed happy at that answer. Then they turned to go. They stopped at the buffet table and picked up some fruit salad and English muffins on their way. When Frank saw them sit down a few tables away, he leaned over to Chet and Joe. "Looks like everyone's heard about your water-skiing skills," he laughed.

"You're the most popular kid here this weekend!" Chet said. "You're going to be on the boat all day today and tomorrow."

"That's okay with me," Joe said. The truth was, he couldn't have been more excited. He hadn't been on a boat since camp last year. All winter he and Frank had talked about this trip, how it would be so cool to be at Lake Poketoe all weekend, with a bunch of their friends. Even though they had to do some school stuff, they were super psyched to go waterskiing and tubing on the lake. And then they could make s'mores around the campfire at night. It wasn't even ten o'clock yet, but already the day was great. It was almost better than he'd imagined.

A few kids at the table next to them stood and

dropped their paper plates in the garbage. Another group had gone down to the lawn below and were throwing a Frisbee. Some others played tag through the trees. Within a few minutes, Mr. Morton came outside. "Has everyone decided? Who will be going to Bucks Mountain to hike?"

A dozen kids raised their hands, then left with Mrs. Rodriguez. She was saying something about bears and rattlesnakes as they walked off. Another big group went inside to do arts and crafts, and soon Mr. Morton's group headed toward the water.

"This is going to be incredible," Ellie said. "I'm so excited!"

"I've never been on a boat before," her redheaded friend, Nina, said.

"Where did you get your water skis?" a boy named Charlie asked.

"Our parents got them for him," Frank said, answering for Joe.

"Now let's get those skis and some life vests," Mr. Morton added.

Frank and Joe led the way to the shed, moving

deeper into the forest. There were log cabins every few yards. Some were just one room, while a few others were two stories high. When they got to the shed, Mr. Morton opened it, then pulled some of the life vests out.

He handed one to each kid, but when he got to Joe, he said, "You put your water skis in the shed last night, right? Why don't you go in and get them?"

Joe peered into the shed. There were only a few life vests there, along with an inner tube and neon-green foam noodles. He pushed inside, moving things around. He knelt down to see if his skis had fallen, but they weren't on the floor. They weren't anywhere.

"What is it?" Frank asked. He stood in the doorway, his brow furrowed.

"My skis," Joe yelled. "They're gone!"

GONE WITHOUT A TRACE

"They have to be here somewhere," Mr. Morton said, scratching his head. He knelt down, looking at the same exact spot Joe had looked at just seconds before. He shook his head. Then he stood on his tiptoes and checked the top shelf. "Hmmm," he muttered.

Behind him, the rest of the group had started whispering to one another. Charlie leaned over to the girl next to him and said something about the skis being stolen. The girl nodded.

"But who would steal them?" Chet asked, overhearing their conversation. He walked around the back of the shed, checking to see if the skis had been put somewhere else. Joe followed behind, but there was just an old shovel and two rakes.

"Now, now," Mr. Morton said. "Let's not jump to conclusions. Are you sure this is where you put them?"

Joe glanced sideways at his brother. Frank nodded. The sun had been going down when they dropped the skis off, but they were certain it was here. There weren't any other sheds in this part of the woods. There were only lots of cabins and lots of trees.

"I'm very sure," Joe insisted. "Frank and Chet walked me here last night, and I put them inside. I closed the door behind me. They were right there. They were right next to the life vests." He pointed to the spot where he'd left them.

"What are we going to do?" Ellie asked.

"I guess we can't go out on the boat now," Charlie said. A few of the other kids groaned.

"We can still go out . . . you'll just have to go

tubing," Mr. Morton said. "Maybe you'll find the skis tonight and you can water-ski tomorrow."

Joe looked at his brother and frowned. The school trip was only three days long, and now they were losing one whole day. "I can't believe this is happening," Joe said sadly. "I've been excited about this trip for months."

"We'll find them," Frank said. He hadn't seen Joe this upset since the Bandits lost their championship game. He patted his brother on the shoulder, trying to make him feel better.

"Someone must've stolen them," Joe declared. "They didn't just disappear."

Chet looked around at the woods. "But who would do that?" he asked.

"I think I know who," Joe said, his voice sad.

Frank looked at the crowd of kids standing around them. Some had towels slung over their shoulders. A few others had already put on their life vests. "Why don't you take the rest of the group out?" Frank said to Mr. Morton. "Hopefully, by the time you get back, we will have found the skis."

Mr. Morton looked back at the lodge, as if he were considering it. "Okay. . . . If you need anything, Mrs. Pinkelton is right there in the lodge. She'll be there if you need any help."

Ellie frowned as she walked down toward the dock. "Good luck," she said. "We'll miss you out there."

A few of her friends turned to wave too. Some boys moaned about how weird it was that the skis were missing, and a few others wondered who had taken them. Charlie kept saying he couldn't believe it.

"You don't have to stay behind," Frank said, turning to Chet.

Chet smiled. "It's the least I can do. I can't believe this either."

Frank glanced at his brother, who had slumped down against the side of the shed. He looked miserable. "We'll find them," he promised.

"Right," Joe mumbled. "But how?"

THE FIVE *W*S

Frank walked over to his brother and held out his hand. "Come on," he said. "Let's get to work."

Joe grabbed a notebook and pencil from the back pocket of his shorts. He always kept them on him just in case. Sometimes he used them to write down things he remembered about other cases, or funny things he'd seen. Other times he needed them for an investigation like this one.

"The five *Ws*," Joe said. "Who, What, When, Where, and Why."

He scribbled the words down the side of the page. Their dad had taught them that this list was a good way to start investigating a case. Sometimes you knew what was taken, but not where it was taken from. Other times you knew when, but not why.

"Who . . . ," Joe said, annoyed. He wrote down *Adam Ackerman* and underlined it. "That's easy. Case solved."

He turned the notebook around and showed Frank and Chet his answer. Frank just sighed. "Come on," he said. "You know it's never that simple."

Chet furrowed his brow. "Why are you so sure it was Adam?"

Joe crossed his arms over his chest. "When we were getting off the bus, I knocked him in the head with the skis. He said, 'You're going to pay for that, Hardy.' What better way to punish me than to take the skis?"

"You can write down 'maybe' next to his name," Frank said. "But this doesn't seem like something Adam would do. It would be too obvious. He'd know we'd all suspect him."

Joe added *(Maybe)* after Adam's name. He had a feeling Frank was right. But still, he couldn't forget Adam's face as the bully pushed past him and off the bus. He'd seemed so mad. Was he mad enough to take the water skis? Would he really do that?

Frank went into the shed, waving for Chet and

Joe to follow. "Let's stick to the facts for now. Why don't you remind us exactly when you put them in the shed?"

Joe walked over to the place where the life vests were. "I leaned them against these shelves right here. I came in right after we arrived."

"They were taken sometime between six o'clock last night and ten o'clock this morning," Chet added. He pointed to the word *When?* on Joe's paper. Joe wrote down the times.

Joe wrote down notes as he talked. Next to *Where?* he wrote: *Storage shed behind the lodge.* Beneath that, he wrote: *They were leaning against the shelves, on the right side of the shed.*

Frank paced back and forth. "Now let's think of *why*," he said.

"They were expensive," Joe said. "Maybe someone wanted to sell them."

"Or it could be because Adam was mad," Chet added. "Just like you said."

Frank scratched his head. "Maybe someone is playing a joke on you. But that doesn't seem likely."

Joe wrote down all the reasons why someone might've wanted to take the skis. His dad liked to call this a "motive." A motive was a reason why someone would commit a crime.

"*What*," Joe said. "That's easy. My water skis." He wrote down a short description of the skis, including that they were tied with a blue strap. When he was done, he looked down the list. They didn't have much information about this case. If Adam Ackerman hadn't taken the skis, who had?

Chet knelt down by the shed door. He was looking at a yellow towel crumpled on the floor. "Could this be a clue?" he asked.

Frank picked up the towel, noticing it had the letters SLSG written across the top in big black print. "Maybe," he said. "It's hard to tell how long it's been here. I have no idea what 'SLSG' means."

Joe flipped to a clean page in his notebook and wrote down *Yellow towel—SLSG*. "We should probably write down everything in here, just in case," he said. He counted an oar, a life tube, three extra life vests, and the foam noodles. Then he

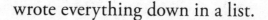

wrote everything down in a list. When he was done, Frank and Chet came to his side, reading over the notes with him. Chet crossed his arms over his chest. "Where should we start?" he asked.

Frank turned and looked out the shed door toward the lodge. The closest cabin to the shed was only a few yards away. The sign in front read PINECONE CABIN. He recognized it instantly.

He stared out over the lake toward Bucks Mountain. Mrs. Rodriguez had left less than half an hour ago. He'd seen Adam and Paul go with her. Maybe it was unlikely that Adam had taken the skis, but that was the same cabin he'd seen Paul and Adam go into last night. Besides, it was their only real lead.

Frank pointed at the path that led into the woods. "Let's go that way," he said. "If we're fast, we can probably catch Mrs. Rodriguez's group before they get to the other side of the lake."

Chet followed behind as Joe and Frank took off down the trail. "I'm confused. . . . Why do we want to catch them?" he called out.

"Adam's in that group," Frank said.

"I thought you didn't think it was him," Chet said.

Frank ran faster, waving for Chet to hurry up. "It probably wasn't. But if he's the only one on our suspect list, we might as well be sure. Once we know he didn't steal them—"

"Then we can find out who did," Joe finished. He smiled as he ran past his brother, moving deeper into the woods.

THEY'RE HIDING SOMETHING

They'd been running for a while when they spotted the group up ahead. The kids, led by Mrs. Rodriguez, turned and took the trail down toward the beach. Frank and Joe could see Adam and Paul in the back, walking along behind the others. The two boys were each carrying a stick, which they used to swat away the tree branches.

"Hey!" Frank called out. "Wait for us!"

The whole group turned around, studying the

boys. Mrs. Rodriguez smiled. "Where did you boys come from? I thought you were going out on the boat today," she said. "Is everything all right?"

When Frank, Joe, and Chet finally caught up, they were out of breath. "We're fine. Mr. Morton said we could hang around the lodge as long as Mrs. Pinkelton knew where we were. We aren't going on the hike," Joe said. "We were just hoping to talk to Adam for a second."

Mrs. Rodriguez nodded. "I guess that's fine. Be careful, though—you missed my warning. There are rattlesnakes in these woods. There are also brown bears. I don't think we'll run into one, but make sure you make a lot of noise. The last thing we want is to sneak up on one."

The group started back down the trail. Frank noticed that a few kids in the front had sticks too. They banged them together as they walked, making noise.

"What do you want?" Adam asked. He didn't look at them as he talked.

"We just wanted to ask you a few questions," Chet said.

Adam and Paul laughed. "Is this for another one of your little mysteries?"

Joe took a deep breath to calm himself down. He didn't like how Adam said those words. He was always making fun of the Hardys, even when he didn't mean to. "We know you took my skis," Joe said. "Where did you put them?"

Adam scrunched his nose. "Your skis? What are you talking about?"

Frank glanced sideways at his brother. Joe was letting Adam get to him. Just because Adam and Paul were staying in the cabin near the shed, that didn't mean Adam definitely had taken the skis. It didn't mean anything that he had been rude to Joe, either.

Frank tried a different strategy. "We noticed your cabin was near the storage shed. Did you see anything strange last night?"

Paul laughed. "What are you guys even talking about?"

"Joe's water skis are missing," Chet explained. "And yesterday, on the bus, you got really mad at him. You told him you'd get back at him for hitting you with his skis."

Adam rubbed his head like he didn't remember. "Oh . . . that."

Joe was so mad, his cheeks were red. "Did you take them? Don't lie to us."

Adam shook his head. "I didn't, I swear."

Paul stopped walking. He turned, looking at Frank and Joe for the first time. "We definitely didn't take them. When Adam said that, we were going to play a prank on you or something. Pull your chair out when you tried to sit down. Something like that."

Frank stepped toward his brother. He was starting to feel really annoyed. Why did Adam always have to be so mean?

"Well, if you didn't take them," Chet said, "who did?"

"Look, we didn't see anything weird," Adam said. "I don't know anything about this."

Paul stood still. He looked at Frank and Joe like he wanted to say something, but he didn't. Then

Adam nudged him. "Come on, let's go," he said, pulling Paul along behind him.

Adam and Paul turned, following the rest of the group up the path.

"That was weird," Chet said. "Didn't it seem like Paul wanted to tell us something?"

"Definitely," Joe said. "He knows something."

Frank sighed. "It's like he was afraid to say it in front of Adam."

The boys walked back toward the shed. Joe looked down at his notebook, going through all the clues they had. It was possible the person who took the skis had something to do with the yellow towel, but they couldn't be sure. Now the best thing to do would be to go back to the shed and see if there was anything they'd missed.

They hadn't gotten very far when they heard footsteps behind them. They turned and saw Paul running toward them. He looked nervous.

"Hey, guys," he said. "I don't have much time, but I wanted to tell you I did see something. Last night I got out of bed and saw a boy walking down toward the lake with your skis. I just thought it was you."

"What did he look like?" Joe asked.

"He had on a black hooded sweatshirt," Paul said. "He had your skis—I saw them."

"Are you sure?" Frank asked.

"Positive," Paul said.

Frank looked at Joe and smiled. Maybe it hadn't been such a bad idea to start with Adam. It wasn't even eleven o'clock and they already had a break in the case. Paul Alcotti was now their very first witness.

THE SUSPECT

Joe flipped his notebook to a clean page. He wrote the word *Who?* again, and *Possible suspect* beside it. "Tell us everything you remember," Joe said.

Paul rubbed his hands together like he was nervous. He glanced over his shoulder. The group was behind him, moving along a trail by the beach. "Umm . . ."

Frank saw how worried Paul seemed. Adam was at the back of the group. He hadn't noticed Paul was gone yet.

"If you don't want anyone to know you told us, that's okay," Frank said. "We can keep it a secret."

Paul nodded. "Yeah, I just . . . I don't want Adam know I'm helping you guys. He'd be mad, you know?"

"It's okay," Frank said. Their dad had taught them that sometimes witnesses didn't like anyone to know they'd helped with a case. Maybe it was because they knew the suspect, or maybe they were scared the suspect might get mad at them. Mr. Hardy told Frank and Joe it was okay to keep what they said a secret.

"So we were hanging out in our cabin. And I got out of bed and went to the bathroom," Paul began. "I was looking out the window and I saw this kid. He was walking out of the shed with the skis. I didn't think it was weird at first, but then when you said someone had stolen them . . ."

Chet put his hands on his hips. "That's crazy!" he said. "Who was this guy? What did he look like?"

Paul rubbed his head. "Like I said, he had a black

hooded sweatshirt on. He was wearing jeans. I think he had light hair . . . like blond. And he looked short."

Joe wrote down everything Paul said. "Do you remember what time it was?"

Paul bit his lip. "Maybe nine thirty. It was just after lights-out—that I remember."

"Where was he heading?" Frank asked. "Did you see where he went?"

"He was going toward the dock . . . ," Paul said. He opened his mouth to say something else, but then someone called out from the forest behind him.

"Paul! Where'd you go? Are you there?"

Paul's eyes went wide when he heard Adam's voice. "I gotta go!" he said, turning to run back. "I'll see you guys later!"

The boys watched as Paul ran back toward the group. "I'm coming!" he called out to Adam. "I just got lost!"

Within a few seconds he was gone. Frank turned to Joe. "We officially have a suspect," he said. "We're getting closer, I can feel it. Hopefully, we'll find your skis and be out on the lake this afternoon."

Joe smiled. "I hope," he said. "Let's go back to the shed and see if we missed anything. We have to find that boy."

Ten minutes later Frank, Chet, and Joe were back at the shed. They walked around it, looking for any clues they might have missed.

"Nine thirty," Chet mumbled. "The thief was out late. He must've waited until everyone was in their bunks for the night."

Joe stopped by a corner of the shed. He barely heard what Chet had just said. He was too busy studying some tracks that led down to the beach. "Look at these," he said. "We must've missed them before."

Frank came around the side of the shed. There was one long line that started a few yards away. "The edge of the skis must've dug into the dirt," he said, following it.

They walked beside the tracks, noticing that they went toward the dock. Halfway to the dock the lines changed. There were two lines, not one.

They were about a foot away from each other.

"He started by carrying them," Frank said. "That's why there were no lines. Then he dragged them together. Then he took them apart and dragged one in each hand."

Chet knelt down. He picked something blue out of a pile of dead leaves. "Is this something?" he asked.

Joe perked up when he saw the blue strap. "That's what held the skis together!" he said. "We're definitely close."

Chet passed the blue strap to Joe, who put it in his pocket. They followed the tracks all the way down to the beach, where they ended right at the dock. There were a few girls swimming in the water. Another group was sitting in a speedboat, reading. One of the girls, in a pink sundress, was weaving a friendship bracelet with colorful string. Behind them, an older woman in a giant white hat thumbed through a magazine.

Frank stopped before the girls noticed them. "This might be it," he said. "Maybe the thief used this boat to water-ski. That would make sense, right?"

Before Joe could answer, the girl in the pink sundress turned around. She was a little older than the boys, maybe ten. "What's up?" she said. She put down the bracelet she was making.

Frank stepped forward. "We were wondering if you've seen a boy in a black hooded sweatshirt and jeans. He was definitely wearing those last night, and maybe even today, too. He has light hair and is pretty short."

The girl just shrugged. One of her friends was lying out on a yellow towel. Another one was drinking a soda.

"I didn't see anyone like that," the girl in the sundress said. "But we just got here last night."

"What time?" Frank asked.

"Like eight o'clock," another girl said. "This is our first day here, and it's been quiet all morning."

"Is this the only boat at this dock?" Chet asked.

"There's been a few boats going in and out," the girl said.

Joe wrote down what she said in his notebook. He was glad Chet had asked her that question. Just because the thief took the skis down to this dock didn't mean he got on this boat. He could have used any of the boats that left from here.

"But you didn't see a boy by that description? He might have had water skis with him," Frank said.

Another girl turned around. She was wearing

a yellow sweatshirt with the words SAINT LILAC SCHOOL FOR GIRLS across the front. "There were some boys," she said. "But no one who looked like that. It was dark by the time we got here last night, though."

"Did you see anything strange?" Chet asked.

The girls shook their heads.

Joe let out a deep breath. He knew the boy had probably changed out of whatever he was wearing last night. They'd have better luck if they questioned people at the lodge. But who would remember seeing a boy in a black sweatshirt? Half the third- and fourth-grade boys from Bayport Elementary were wearing dark sweatshirts last night.

"Thanks," Joe said. "Let us know if you remember anything. We're staying back there." He pointed to the lodge.

The boys turned and walked back to the lodge, more confused than ever.

"The lines lead right to the dock," Chet pointed out. "He must've brought the skis there."

"But he could be anyone," Frank said. "We don't

have a good enough description of him. Paul saw him from so far away."

Joe scanned the woods. "We have to have missed something," he said.

Frank looked around. "Yeah," he agreed. "But what?"

MISTAKEN IDENTITY

Frank knew something wasn't right. Sometimes he got a nagging feeling that they'd asked the wrong questions, or that they were looking in the wrong places. There was something about this case that they had missed.

The boys walked through the woods in silence. Frank glanced up the hill, noticing the cabin Adam and Paul had stayed in. It said PINECONE CABIN above the door. Paul hadn't given them a great description. But where had he been standing? Had he seen everything clearly?

"I just want to check something," Frank said, walking toward it.

When he got there, the front door was open. He crept inside, Chet and Joe following close behind him. There were four bedrooms spread out off the main living area.

"Paul said he was staying in that room in the corner," Joe whispered. He had his notebook out and was looking at his notes.

"Which means he probably used the bathroom that's right near it," Chet said.

The three boys climbed the stairs. The cabin was much dirtier than the main lodge. There were some cobwebs near the ceilings, and mud tracked across the floor. When they got upstairs, they went into the tiny bathroom. There was only one window, and it was covered with dirt.

"He saw the boy from here? At night?" Chet asked. "It's the middle of the day and I can barely see out of this window!"

Frank leaned forward, putting his nose close to the glass. "Exactly," he said.

"Whatever he saw," Joe added, "it can't be trusted."

Frank stood up straight. "He probably did see someone in a black hooded sweatshirt," he said. "He'd be able to tell his height."

Joe's eyes widened. He cupped his hand over his mouth, like he'd just remembered something. "I know what we missed!" he said. "It all makes sense now."

"What?" Chet asked.

"SLSG!" Joe said. "The yellow towel!"

Frank and Chet almost laughed. "Huh?" Frank said. "What about it?"

Joe was so excited, he started talking twice as fast as normal. "When we went down to the dock and saw those girls. One of them was sitting on a yellow towel. And the other girl was wearing a sweatshirt that said Saint Lilac School for Girls."

"Wait . . . SLSG," Frank repeated. He couldn't help but smile. Joe had figured it out. They'd missed one important clue. "The towel from the shed belonged to a girl."

Chet looked confused. "I don't understand," he said.

"SLSG stands for Saint Lilac School for Girls," Joe said. "The girls only got to the lake last night. So whoever left the towel in the shed was there between eight o'clock last night and ten o'clock this morning. Right when the water skis were stolen."

"This whole time we've been looking for a boy in a hooded sweatshirt," Frank said. "And Paul didn't even see the person clearly."

Chet laughed. "I can't believe it!" he said. "We've been looking for a boy . . . when we should've been looking for a girl!"

"Exactly," Joe said. "We need to go back to the dock and talk to those girls again, before it's too late."

Joe ran down the stairs, more excited than ever. They were getting so close to solving the case. Maybe they didn't know who their suspect was, but at least they knew what school she went to, and who she was hanging out with. With a little luck, they'd be out water-skiing by the end of the day.

THE NEW GIRL

By the time the boys got back to the dock, the girls were packing up their things. One girl stuffed her towel and book in a straw bag. Another pulled some neon foam noodles out of the water.

"Hey, Annie, can you pass me my magazines?" one of the girls asked.

As a girl in a sundress turned to grab the magazines, she saw the boys.

"It's you guys again," Annie said. "Did you find that kid?"

"Well . . . ," Frank started. "We may have made a mistake. We don't think it's a boy we're looking for. We think it's a girl. And we think she goes to your school."

Annie frowned. "What do you mean?"

A few of her friends had climbed out of the water and onto the dock. They were drying off while they listened to what the boys were saying. One girl raised her eyebrows.

"We might have gotten things confused," Joe said. He stopped there, not wanting to tell them too much. There was a chance their suspect was one of the girls they were talking to.

He looked around, studying the girls' faces. They all seemed nice enough. Then he noticed their hair. There were eight of them standing around the dock, but only two of them had light hair. Both of those two girls were taller than most girls their age.

Earlier, Paul had described the suspect as being

short with light hair, and the boys had agreed that that was probably right, even if it was dark and the window was dirty. He still would've been able to see how tall she was. Was it okay to tell the girls more? Could they risk it?

Before Joe could decide, Chet blurted out another question. "Did you see a girl with water skis?"

Frank glanced sideways at his brother. This was sometimes the problem with having friends help during a case. They didn't always know which parts of the story they shouldn't share with people.

"We think the girl in the black hooded sweatshirt may have taken a pair of water skis," Joe explained. "Does any of this sound familiar?"

Annie started laughing. "I knew she was up to something!" she said.

A girl with a black braid added, "I can't believe this is happening."

"What?" Frank asked. "Who are you talking about?"

Annie sat down on the dock. "And she was being so weird last night," she remembered. Then she turned to the boys. "I think you're looking for the new girl . . . Trixie? No, wait, it's Trina."

Joe pulled out his notebook and wrote down the names with a question mark next to each one. "Why do you think it's her? She's short with light hair?"

"And she was acting so weird last night!" the girl with the braid said. "She's always acting weird, but this was different."

Frank scratched his head. "What do you mean? Did you see her with the water skis?"

"No . . . but that doesn't matter. Everyone else was playing board games in our cabin," Annie said. "And out of nowhere, Trina and this other girl said they had to leave. But they wouldn't tell us where they were going."

Joe wrote down all the details, nodding. It did sound like strange behavior. "So the girls went together? Do you remember her friend's name?"

The girl with the black braid answered, "Well . . . I doubt they're friends. The other girl is named Sara Carter."

A few of the other girls giggled. Frank glanced sideways at his brother. It was starting to seem like the rest of the girls didn't like Trina very much. He felt bad that they were laughing at her behind her back.

"It's just . . . ," Annie said. "Trina doesn't have many friends. She's only been at school a week."

"Do any of you know her?" Frank asked.

The girls shook their heads. "No . . . not really," Annie said.

"Do you know where she is right now?" Chet said.

A girl with pigtails told the boys, "We haven't seen her since this morning."

"I saw her!" a redheaded girl said. "Right after breakfast. She was by our cabin."

Joe wrote down *Last seen near SLSG cabin*. Then he asked, "Where is your cabin? Does it have a name?"

"We're in the Oaks," Annie said. She slung her polka-dotted towel around her shoulder as she spoke. Then she pointed into the woods. "It's the red cabin. It's a five-minute walk that way."

Frank looked at Chet and his brother, then back out over the lake. The sun was high in the sky, and it was close to noon. But Mr. Morton hadn't come back yet with the boat and the rest of the group. "We should go to that cabin now," Frank said. "We still have a lot to figure out."

The boys thanked the Saint Lilac girls and

headed off into the woods. "There are still so many questions about the motive," Joe said, looking down at his notebook. "Even if it is Trina, we still don't know why she did it. What would she want with my water skis?"

"Be careful," Frank said. "We don't actually know if it's Trina, remember? The girls didn't see her with the skis."

Joe flipped through his notes again. Reading through them, he realized Frank was right. They'd asked if the girls had seen Trina with the skis, but they hadn't. The girls were only certain of a few things: that she was acting weird, that she didn't have a lot of friends, and that they didn't know her.

"But if they don't know her, why do they think she was acting weird? How would they know that?" Joe asked.

Frank nodded. "And if they're not friends with her or they don't like her very much, they might think she did something she didn't do."

Chet turned back to look at the lake as they walked. "We'll get to the bottom of this," he said.

"By tomorrow we'll be out on the lake, water-skiing with our friends."

"I hope," Frank said.

But as Joe looked back at the sun in the sky, he wasn't so sure. How could they know if it was Trina who'd taken the skis? And even if she had taken them, where were they now? Would Joe ever see them again?

TWISTS AND TURNS

When they got to the red cabin, there were two girls sitting on the deck. One had a giant bowl of grapes, and another was eating the last of her cheeseburger. The one with the grapes had reddish-brown hair, and the other had dark eyes and black hair. Neither of them fit the description of Trina.

"We were hoping you could help us," Frank said, climbing up the stairs. "Do you know a girl named Trina? She's new to your school?"

The girl with black hair narrowed her eyes. "The only girl who's new is named Tamara. Is that who you mean?"

Before Frank could respond, the girl got up and went to the door. "Tamara!" she called inside. "Someone is looking for you!"

Within minutes, a short girl with a blond bob came to the door. She looked confused. "Who's looking for me?" she asked. "What's wrong?"

Joe stepped forward. "I'm Joe and this is my brother, Frank. We're from Bayport Elementary," he explained. "We're staying at another cabin on the lake, on the other side of the woods. We were hoping to ask you some questions."

Tamara shrugged. "Sure. I guess that's fine. What's wrong?"

The two other girls went back to their snacks. They started talking about joining the Saint Lilac basketball team. Tamara came outside and sat down on the deck stairs. She put her chin in her hands.

"We heard you're new in school," Frank said. "Is that true?"

Tamara looked puzzled. "Yeah . . . why?"

"We're trying to solve a mystery," Chet said. "And we've been going around, asking if anyone saw anything strange. Someone said you might know something."

"Who?" Tamara asked.

Chet pointed back to the dock. "Just some of the girls down by the dock. They told us your name was Trina."

"They don't even know my name," Tamara said sadly. "What did they say about me?"

"What were you doing last night after eight o'clock?" Joe asked. "Were you here, in your cabin?"

Tamara scratched her head. "Yeah . . . I think so. We got in around eight thirty, and then everyone had dinner together. Then some people were hanging out. I took a walk, but that's about it."

Joe looked at his brother. It didn't seem like Tamara was trying to hide anything. If she had stolen the skis, it would be odd for her to admit that she'd left the cabin last night. "Did you see anything strange?" he asked.

"No," she said. "My friend and I were just walking and talking. I just didn't want to be around everybody last night. I felt like people were laughing at me."

She looked sad when she said it. Joe was going to ask another question, but then he noticed a girl looking out the window of the cabin. She had light blond pigtails. "Is that your friend?" he said.

Tamara turned around and waved at the girl. "Yeah, that's Sara. She's been really nice to me since I've gotten here. She's the one I went on the walk with."

Frank turned back to Tamara. "We're looking for a pair of water skis," he said. "Do you know anything about that?"

Tamara shook her head. "No. Who lost them?"

"We think they were stolen," Joe said. "They were mine."

"I'm sorry about that," Tamara said. "That's such a bummer. I used to water-ski in my old town. I used to live right on a lake. I really loved it."

"Yeah, it's the best," Joe added. He kept looking

at Sara. She was still watching them from the window. She looked curious as she watched them talk.

Then Sara opened the window. "Tamara!" she called. "We need your help with something! Can you come here?"

Tamara turned back toward the cabin. "I guess I have to go," she said. She smiled at the boys. "Good luck with everything. I hope you find your skis."

With that, she ran up the stairs. The boys walked a few feet away, where the other girls couldn't hear them. "It definitely felt like Tamara was telling the truth," Chet said. "She didn't seem like she has anything to hide."

"I agree," Frank said. "I'm more interested in Sara. . . ."

Joe turned back toward the house. Sara was still at the window. She walked away when she noticed him. "Did you see she has blond hair?" Joe asked.

"She and Tamara look very similar," Frank said. "And she doesn't look very tall either. Which means . . ."

"She could've been the one that Paul saw!" Chet said.

Frank walked ahead of them, into the woods. He waved for them to come hide behind a big tree. "I have an idea," he said.

Chet and Joe crouched down beside him. Chet peered back toward the cabin. The two girls who were sitting on the deck had gone inside.

"If our suspicions are right," Frank said, "Sara is worried about us. And when a suspect is worried they might get caught, they sometimes get sloppy."

"Like the time we caught Lester Pinks," Joe said. Lester had been taking tickets from Fun World, an arcade in Bayport. He'd gotten so nervous after Frank and Joe questioned him that he started covering his tracks. Frank and Joe had been watching him and saw where he'd hidden all the prizes.

"Exactly," Frank said. "We should wait here. I have a hunch that if Sara was the one who took the skis, she'll make her next move soon."

The boys sat down behind the big tree, leaning their backs against it. Time was going by. They only had an hour before they had to be back for lunch. After a while Joe got tired. His eyes started to close, and he fell fast asleep.

"Joe! Wake up! Look!" Frank whispered.

Joe rubbed his eyes. He wasn't sure how long he'd been napping. He peered out from behind the tree. Sara was crawling out from underneath the deck of the cabin. "What happened?" he asked.

"She just went under there. . . . She must be hiding something," Chet said.

Sara looked around the woods before she turned toward the lake. Then she took off down a trail.

"Come on," Frank said. He rushed toward the cabin. When he got to the deck he crawled underneath it, feeling around beneath the dead leaves.

"What's there?" Joe asked. "Did you find anything?"

Frank moved farther under the deck. The light outside the cabin came through the slats in the deck. He could see one ski, but not the other. He pushed the dead leaves and dirt around, but he still couldn't find the other one. It wasn't there.

He crawled back out and handed the ski to Joe. "My ski!" Joe cried.

"Where's the other one?" Chet asked.

"It's not under there," Frank said. He pointed toward the path where Sara had gone. "We have to find her. She knows what happened, and she probably knows where that other ski is."

Joe hid his one ski under the deck again, and the three boys took off through the woods. They ran as fast as they could. By the time they saw Sara up ahead, they were almost out of breath. "Wait! Stop! We need to talk to you!"

Sara turned back, but when she saw who was following her, she started running. She darted down the path toward the beach.

"She's getting away!" Chet cried. "We have to stop her!"

The boys ran even faster. They jumped over fallen trees and rocks. They followed her left through the woods, then right.

Finally she turned toward the beach. The dock was on one side of her, and they were on the other. Sara finally stopped and sat down in the sand.

"We just want to ask you something," Joe panted, out of breath from running. "We think you might be able to help us find the skis."

Sara put her hands up and looked sad. "I'm sorry," she said. Her eyes were brimming with tears. "I can explain, I swear. . . ."

THE HARDY BOYS—and
YOU!

CAN YOU SOLVE THE MYSTERY OF THE MISSING SKIS?

Grab a piece of paper and write your answers down. Or just turn the page to find out!

1. Frank and Joe came up with a list of suspects. Can you think of more? List your suspects.

2. Which clues helped you to solve this mystery? Write them down.

A FRIEND IN NEED

Sara put her face in her hands. For a moment, Frank and Joe almost felt bad for her.

"I'm sorry," she said again. "I really am. I didn't mean to."

"What happened?" Joe asked.

The boys stood there, looking at Sara. Out on the lake, they could see the light of a boat coming toward them. Joe wondered if it was Mr. Morton and the rest of the group, but they were too far away to see.

Sara let out a deep breath. "I was just trying to help Tamara. She's new, and she's been having a really hard time. Some of the girls are mean to her. Last night she was upset, and we went for a walk. She was talking about her old town, and things she liked to do there—"

"And she mentioned waterskiing," Frank said. He remembered Tamara saying she lived on a lake.

"Yeah," Sara said. "She said she was really good at it. And it was this fun thing she used to do with her sisters. So I had this idea to find some water skis so that when we went out on the boat today, she'd be able to show off a little. I knew the other girls would think she was really cool."

Joe scratched his head. Sara's story was starting to make sense, except for one thing. "Why did you take *my* skis? And what happened to the other one?"

"I didn't realize they were yours until after you came to our cabin," Sara said. "Tamara told me you were asking about them, and that's when I realized.

I didn't know, I promise I didn't. They were in the shed with all the life vests. I just thought they were part of the supplies for the different cabins."

Frank nodded. "Why did you take the skis late at night, though?"

Sara put her chin in her hands. "I just wanted it to be a surprise. I snuck out after Tamara went to sleep. I brought the skis down to the boat . . . and that's when it happened."

She bit her lip, like she was afraid to go on.

"What is it?" Joe asked. "What's wrong?"

Sara's eyes filled with tears. "I'm really sorry," she said. "I brought the skis down to the boat, but when I went to put them inside it, one fell. Before I could jump in and get it, it started floating out into the lake. It was so dark . . . I lost it."

Joe let out a deep breath. It was even worse news than when he had found out the skis were gone. This meant one was gone forever. It wasn't stolen, or lost . . . it was somewhere out on the lake. He'd never see it again. What good were water skis if you only had one?

Sara started to cry now. "I'm really sorry," she said, looking at Joe. "I really am."

Joe knew that she was. She looked more upset than ever. He tried to remind himself that she'd only been trying to help her friend. She'd wanted to cheer up Tamara. "It's okay," he said. "I know you were trying to do something good."

Sara stared at her feet. "I hid the other ski because I was hoping . . . ," she said. "I don't know. I was hoping someone would find it or something."

"At least we know what happened now," Frank said.

Chet was staring at the lake. The boat with the light was getting closer. He waved to his dad, who was steering it. "You're back!" he called.

Mr. Morton pulled into the dock. A few kids got out. Some of them were red from being in the sun all morning. Others had towels slung around their necks. "We missed you guys!" Ellie said as she stepped out of the boat. "It wasn't the same without you."

"We have some good news and some bad news," Mr. Morton said. "Which one do you want first?"

Joe glanced sideways at his brother. "The good news?" he said, feeling suddenly nervous.

"We found something of yours," Mr. Morton said, and smiled. He held up the missing water ski.

"My ski!" Joe cried. He took it from Mr. Morton's hand. "This is amazing!"

Mr. Morton continued, "But you haven't heard the bad news yet. We only found one. It was floating out on the lake . . . all alone."

"He only needs one!" Frank laughed. He patted his brother on the back. Joe was practically jumping up and down, he was so excited.

"What do you mean?" Mr. Morton asked. The rest of the group looked confused.

Chet laughed. "It's a long story," he said. "We can tell it to you at lunch."

The boys started up the shore, Sara following close behind them. Joe kept looking at the water ski in his hand. He couldn't believe he'd really gotten it back.

"It's your lucky day," Frank whispered to him.

Joe was smiling so much, his face hurt. "It really is," he said.

"WOOO-HOOOO!" Joe cried. "THIS IS AMAZING!!"

The wind whipped through his hair. He zipped over the water, holding on tight to the handle. All the kids in the boat cheered.

It was Sunday morning, and they had one whole day to be on the water. The boat was packed. Frank, Chet, Sara, and Tamara had all come along for the ride. Joe had let Tamara go first. She turned out to be a great water-skier. She didn't fall once.

Suddenly Joe found himself losing speed and let go of the handles. As the boat slowed down to come back and pick him up, he floated in the water. His life vest came up around his chin, and he bobbed in the cool lake. When the boat circled back to Joe, he grinned.

"This has been one of the best days ever," he declared.

Frank reached down, helping his brother up the metal ladder. Joe grabbed a towel from the bench and sat beside him. "You bet it is. We found your skis, the sun is shining, and we have the whole rest of the day to hang out here before we have to go back home."

"Lake Poketoe is even better than I imagined," Joe said.

The boat picked up speed again. Mr. Morton turned the wheel left, directly into a small wave. All the kids cheered as they bumped up and down in their seats. Frank and Joe cheered the loudest, happy to finally be catching some sunshine.

Chet came over and handed them some iced tea, then got some for himself. He held his glass in the air in a toast. "Good job, guys," he said with a smile. He clinked it against theirs. "Another case solved!"

TALENT SHOW TRICKS

Chapter 1

OPENING ACT

Nine-year-old Frank Hardy sat in the school auditorium, going over a big checklist in a binder.

"Hey, Frank!" Chet Morton, Frank's best friend, waved from the stage. "Check this out!" Chet held up three microphones and pretended to juggle them. "Maybe I can be in the talent show too!"

Frank laughed. He'd been chosen as a Bayport Backstage Buddy member for the school's yearly talent show. That meant he was going to help with anything people needed during the show and make sure everything ran smoothly. He even had his own walkie-talkie to help him communicate with everyone around the auditorium. Mrs. Castle, the music and arts teacher who directed the show, said she picked Frank to work with her because he was so organized and reliable. He didn't want to let her or the students in the show down!

The kids in the show, including his eight-year-old brother, Joe, were in the restrooms, changing into their costumes. Rehearsal would start in just a few minutes. It was Monday, and the show was at the end of the week, so they had a lot of work to do!

Frank took a few moments to check in with the rest of the BBB crew. First he talked through the walkie-talkie with Eli Ramsay, who was helping to work the lights up in a booth above the stage, and made sure he was ready to go. Then he checked on Chet, who was at the back of the auditorium. Chet was going to help with the sound—making sure each act had the right music and making sure the microphones all worked.

"Hey, Chet," Frank called out. His friend was half-hidden behind a huge panel with all sorts of buttons and levers. "You ready to go?"

"You bet!" Chet said, flashing Frank a thumbs-up. "You know, this stuff is pretty cool. Maybe I'll be a sound designer someday. Or a DJ!"

Frank grinned. Chet was always picking up new hobbies. As he walked away from the sound booth, he grabbed the walkie-talkie that was clipped to his jeans.

"Come in, Speedy," he said.

The walkie-talkie crackled, and the voice of his friend Speedy Zermeño squawked over the line. "I'm hearing you loud and clear, Frank!"

"How are things looking back there?" he asked. Speedy was also helping backstage, making sure everyone was ready to go before their act.

"We're ready to go when you are!" Speedy said.

Now that he'd checked in with the crew, Frank looked around the auditorium to see if the student director had arrived yet. Olivia Shapiro was an eighth-grade drama student from Bayport Middle

School, which was just down the street. At that moment, Olivia and her seventh-grade assistant, Zoe, came sweeping into the auditorium. Olivia's face was red and both girls were out of breath. It looked like they both ran from the middle school. Plus, although it was a warm day outside, Olivia always insisted on wearing a scarf wrapped dramatically around her neck. Frank had heard her tell Zoe in a rehearsal last week that all the great directors wore scarves.

Olivia took her usual seat in the auditorium with Zoe beside her. Zoe handed her a bottle of water, a notebook, and a pen while Olivia fanned herself.

Frank went up to Olivia. "Everyone's ready to start."

"Thank you, Frank," she said. "Can you call the cast to the stage, please? I want to talk with them before we begin."

"Sure," Frank said. He got Speedy on the walkie-talkie and told her to send the cast out. Slowly, students started to trickle onto the stage. Most were dressed in colorful costumes or fancy clothes. Some held props, like Joe, who was clutching the half-dozen orange balls he juggled in his act. Others carried instruments, like the new kid at Bayport, Ezra Moore, who held his violin and bow.

"Attention, everyone!" Olivia said, waving her hand to get the cast's attention. "I have an announcement to make."

The students stopped their chattering and turned toward their student director.

"I want to remind all of you to have your friends and family book their tickets for Friday's show *now*," Olivia said. "You don't want them to end up without a seat, do you?"

The cast shook their heads.

"Please feel free to see me after today's rehearsal for more tickets if you need them," Mrs. Castle chimed in. She was watching from the back of the auditorium.

"Okay, then. You'll remind them tonight when you get home." Olivia clapped her hands. "Places, please!" Frank saw a few kids roll their eyes. Olivia could be pretty bossy, and not everyone liked that!

The students scattered into the wings at the sides of the stage. The first and last numbers of the evening were songs that Olivia had choreographed herself, and they featured everyone in the show. Frank took his usual place in a seat behind Olivia and Zoe and got out his walkie-talkie.

"Eli," he said. "Can you bring up the lights for the opening number?"

"Roger, boss!" Eli radioed back. The lights in the auditorium dimmed, while those on the stage brightened.

"Chet," Frank asked, "is the music for the opening number ready to go?"

"Whenever you are, Frank," Chet replied.

"Speedy," Frank said, "is everyone in position backstage?"

"We're ready!" she said.

Frank leaned forward to tell Olivia they were ready

to start, but she was deep in conversation with Zoe.

". . . think it's going to be okay," Zoe was saying to Olivia. "I heard Mrs. Castle say that over half the tickets have already been sold."

"*Okay* isn't good enough," Olivia said. "I want to be a professional director someday, and this is my first chance to prove myself. This show *has* to sell out. What happens if they take the show away from me? Then what will I do next year?"

"Um, Olivia?" Frank interrupted. "Everyone's ready to start when you are."

"I'm ready," Olivia said. "Let's go."

"Chet," Frank said into his walkie-talkie, "start the music. Eli, hit the lights. Here we go, everybody!"

WARMING UP

When the opening number was over, Joe walked off the stage with a frown. He did not like to dance, but Olivia had him stepping and jumping and turning all over the stage in the first song, which featured the entire cast of the talent show. At least it was over for now!

Joe followed most of the other acts to Mr. Palmer's classroom, which was just across the hall from the entrance to the backstage. The talent show was using it as a greenroom, the place where acts not performing could hang out while they waited for their turn. Frank stood at the door with a walkie-talkie that connected him to Ellie Freeman. She'd let them know whenever it was time for them to get ready backstage before it was their turn to go on.

Joe sat down at a desk and took a swig from his water bottle. Then he grabbed his juggling balls from his backpack and practiced his routine in his head.

"What happens if you drop one?" Ezra asked as he sat down at the desk beside Joe. Ezra had only been going to Bayport Elementary for about a month. Joe knew him a little because he had recently joined Joe's baseball team, the Bandits.

Joe shrugged. "I just pick them all back up and try again."

Ezra played with the latch on his violin case. "I wish I had a cool talent like yours."

"The violin is cool!" Joe reassured him.

"I hate it," Ezra complained. "I mean, not the violin. I actually like the violin, but I hate the idea of everyone knowing that I play. Almost every school I've gone to, I've been teased for playing. I wish I could just keep it a secret."

Joe frowned. "Then . . . why are you doing the talent show?"

Ezra sighed. "My parents are making me."

"Oh," Joe said.

"Maybe I'll get a cold before Friday," Ezra said, "and I won't have to perform."

"Ezra, it won't be that bad!" Joe reassured his new friend.

"Or maybe the power will go out in the whole school," Ezra continued. "Or my violin will break. Or . . ."

Joe bumped Ezra's shoulder with his own. "Hey, don't worry. You like the violin, right?"

Ezra nodded.

"Then that's all that matters!" Joe said. "Besides, you play really well. No one will make fun of you when they hear how awesome you are."

Just then Adam Ackerman, the school's biggest bully, stuck his head into the greenroom.

"Hey, nerds!" he said. "How's your stupid show going?"

Joe just rolled his eyes, but he could see that Ezra was upset. He hadn't yet learned to ignore Adam the way most of them had.

"Keep moving, Adam," Ellie said. "What are you even doing here after school is out?"

"I bet he had detention," Joe said. A couple of kids giggled.

"As a matter of fact, I *did*. Detention's the only reason I'd hang out at this school after the bell. Not like you geeks." Adam cast his eyes over everyone in the room, looking for something else to make fun of. His eyes landed on Ezra and his violin case. He started to laugh. "You play the violin, Moore? Wow. And I actually thought you might be cool."

Ezra gave Joe a defeated look.

"Hey, leave him alone," Joe said.

"Yeah, Adam! We all know you're only jealous," Ellie added, "because when you auditioned for the show, Mrs. Castle wouldn't let you in."

A couple of people around the room gasped, while others laughed or hid their smiles. Joe wondered what Adam's talent had been. He'd have to ask Ellie later.

Adam's face turned red.

"Yeah, well, I hope your stupid talent show is a disaster!" he yelled.

BUBBLE TROUBLE

At the beginning of rehearsal the next day, Olivia asked Frank to gather the cast. With the help of Speedy and Ellie, soon they had everyone on the stage, where Olivia was standing with Zoe and a boy who had a notebook in his hand and a pencil tucked behind his ear. Frank recognized him from the hallways, but he was a in a different class, so Frank didn't know his name.

"Attention, everyone!" Olivia said. When everyone

was looking at her, she motioned to the boy beside her with a flourish. "This is Diego Mendez. If you don't know him already, he's one of the writers for the school paper. He's here to write a very special article about the talent show. Let's give him a round of applause."

The cast clapped for Diego, who bowed his head.

"Diego, would you like to say a few words?" Olivia asked.

"Sure," he said, taking a step toward the group. "Thanks for letting me watch your rehearsal today! It's going to help me write a really great article about the show."

"We're going to be famous!" Joe exclaimed.

The cast laughed, and Frank shook his head. Joe loved to be the center of attention!

Olivia told everyone to get into their places for the opening number. After Frank told her everyone was ready to start, he went to the back of the auditorium. Olivia raised her hands and shouted "Action!" just like a movie director.

Frank looked down at the binder open in his lap. His job as the Backstage Buddy to the stage manager, Mrs. Castle, was to help keep everything from the lights and sound to the entrances and exits of the cast running smoothly. It was a big job, and he had every step of it written down in front of him.

He got on the walkie-talkie and told Eli to dim the lights in the audience and bring them up on the stage. Then he told Chet to start the music for the opening number. Once the music began, he radioed Speedy, who was in the wings, and had her send the dancers who were waiting there out onto the stage. The show had only started, and already Frank was nervous! There was a lot to do.

They ran through the first few acts, took a small break, and then went on with the rest of the show. Every now and then, when Frank had a moment to relax, he would sneak glances at Diego. He wondered what the older boy was writing about the show in his reporter's notebook. Olivia also seemed very curious. She was leaning so far forward in her chair to try to get a peek that she nearly fell out of her seat.

"Okay, Eli, turn on the spotlight," Frank said over the radio after the Connolly twins had finished their acrobatics routine. "Speedy, send Daniel out."

Daniel Tate, a fourth grader who was in the same class as Frank, walked out onto the stage. He stepped into the bright pool of the spotlight with his gold trumpet held in one hand. He lifted the instrument to his mouth to play "When the Saints Go Marching In" just the way he'd done at every other rehearsal, but Frank could tell something was wrong this time. Daniel blew and blew, but no sound came out of the trumpet.

Daniel frowned as he gave his trumpet a little shake. He put the trumpet up to his lips again, took a giant breath, and then blew with all his might. His cheeks puffed out and his face turned red, but no sound came out. . . .

Instead a stream of soapy bubbles exploded from the bell of the instrument!

For a moment, everyone just stared in shock. Then the auditorium went crazy. Frank could see

Eli burst into laughter. Onstage, Daniel shook his trumpet some more and then tried to play it again, which made more bubbles come floating out of it. He started to laugh along with the others. Olivia screeched and bolted out of her seat.

"What is going on here?" she demanded. "Is this a joke, Daniel? The show is in three days, and I don't think this is funny!"

"It's not a joke!" Daniel said. "I swear! I don't know what's happening!"

"Frank!" Olivia barked. "Stop the show!"

Frank nodded and got on the radio. "Eli, turn on the lights in the auditorium."

As the lights rose around them, Olivia started to march down the aisle toward the stage with Zoe on her heels.

"Where are you going?" Frank called after them.

"I'm getting to the bottom of this!" Olivia said back over her shoulder.

Diego, who only minutes before had been slumped in his seat, looking a little bored, was scribbling furiously in his notebook as he jumped up to follow Olivia. Frank went after them and caught them onstage, where Olivia was questioning Daniel.

"You *swear* you didn't do this, Daniel?" she asked him.

"I swear on my favorite stack of Car Racer games!" Daniel said, holding up one hand. His eyes were wide and he looked a little nervous. "I warmed up before rehearsal started, and it was playing just fine."

"Could anyone else have messed with the trumpet between then and now?" Olivia asked. It was exactly the same question Frank would have asked. His father was a private investigator, and he'd taught Frank and Joe practically everything he knew.

"I don't know," Daniel said. "I put it back in its case before the opening number and got it out again just now. I guess someone could have done something to it in between."

"Where's the case?" Olivia asked.

"In the hall," Daniel said. "I'll show you."

He led them offstage, through the wings, and into the hallway just outside the auditorium. This was where a lot of kids in the cast had left their things because there wasn't enough space in the greenroom for everyone's stuff. Backpacks lined the hall, along with some books and stray props for the show. Most of the props were right off the wings backstage, but not all. Daniel led them to a brown rectangular case sitting between a blue gym bag and a pair of black tap shoes.

"Here it is," Daniel said. He opened the case.

Everyone gasped.

Inside was a bottle of Mr. Fantastic's Wonder Bubbles from Mr. Fun's Joke Shop, and a note:

This is just the beginning. I won't stop until the talent show is canceled!

ON THE CASE

"Who do you think could have messed with Daniel's trumpet?" Joe asked. He and Frank were in the woods behind their house, on the way to their secret tree house. Their dad had built it for them, and it was perfectly hidden in the trees. You'd never see it if you didn't already know it was there. Joe grabbed the rope that was tucked behind the trunk of a tree and gave a tug, which released the hidden rope ladder. He and Frank climbed the ladder into the tree house.

"I don't know," Frank said, "but it looks like we have a case to solve!"

The tree house wasn't just a cool place to hang out. It was also the headquarters for Frank and Joe's investigations. It was their top-secret place where they looked over clues and talked over any theories they had on each case.

"We've got some pretty good clues already," Joe said. "Did you grab the note you found in the trumpet case?"

Frank pulled the piece of paper out of his pocket and handed it to Joe. "Sure did. Take a look."

Joe looked at the note, taking in every detail just like his father had taught him. The paper was from a school notebook, the edges frayed from being torn out. The words were written in pencil and in block letters that disguised the handwriting.

Joe stared at the note. He still couldn't believe it. Who would want to ruin the talent show?

A part of him was excited, though. He and Frank had been solving mysteries around Bayport for a while now, and Joe loved solving mysteries more than anything else. More than video games, macaroni and cheese, or even baseball!

"Once we found the note, Diego started asking a bunch of questions, and Mrs. Castle decided to cancel rehearsal for the afternoon," Frank said. "So, what do you think? Want to try to figure out who's behind this?"

"You bet I do!" Joe said.

They had a special notebook that they used to keep track of clues, theories, and the Five Ws. The Five Ws was a set of questions their father had taught them about. Finding the answers to the Five Ws was the key to solving any mystery.

They started the way they always did, with Joe writing out the Five Ws in the notebook in big letters:

The 5Ws
1. Who?
2. What?
3. When?
4. Where?
5. Why?

"The *what* is Daniel Tate's trumpet," Frank said. "The *where* and *when* are at the talent show rehearsal in the auditorium this afternoon."

Joe wrote all that down. "So we just have to figure out *who* and *why*."

"I bet if we figured out the *why*, it would lead us to the *who*," Joe said.

"Good thinking," Frank replied. "Who has a reason to want the talent show canceled?"

"Well—" Joe started to say.

"Boys!" someone called. Joe recognized the voice as their father's.

Frank opened the trapdoor of the tree house. Fenton Hardy, one of the only people besides Frank and Joe who knew about the secret tree house, was standing below.

"Hey, Dad," Frank said. "What's up?"

"Chet and Iola are here to see you," he said.

"We'll be right there!" Joe said. Then he turned to his brother. "I guess we'll talk about this later."

Frank nodded. "Let's go."

They climbed down from the tree house and met

up with Chet and his younger sister, Iola, in their backyard. Iola was also involved in the talent show; she was going to be singing a song. Frank and Joe ended up doing almost everything with Chet and Iola, since Chet was their best friend and Iola was on the Bandits with them.

"Hey, guys!" Iola said with a wave. "Our parents said we could come over and play until dinner if you want."

"Sounds great!" Joe said. "Want to play kickball? We can do two-on-two."

"Sure!" Iola said.

"Pretty crazy about rehearsal today, huh?" Chet said. "Do you guys have any idea who it might have been?"

Frank shook his head. "Not yet, but we're going to try to find out."

"Whoever it was, they'd better watch out now that you two are on the case!" Iola said.

Joe got an inflatable ball from the shed, and they played Rock, Paper, Scissors to decide the teams. It was Joe and Chet versus Frank and Iola. Frank stood on home plate, and Chet rolled the ball at him. He gave it a huge kick that sent it soaring into the air. While Joe scrambled after the ball, Frank ran the bases, touching a hand to the swing set, the fence, and the biggest oak tree in the yard before running back to home plate. He and Iola high-fived. Their team was off to a great start! The lead changed hands between the two teams several times.

As the sun started to dip below the trees, everyone knew Chet and Iola would have to head home for dinner soon, so the game become even fiercer. It was the last inning, and Frank and Iola were in the lead by one run. Joe was on second base, and Chet was up. If Chet kicked a home run, he and Joe would win the game. Joe chewed on his lower lip nervously. Chet had never been a great athlete. While the others all played on the

Bandits baseball team, Chet had always preferred to pursue one of his ever-changing hobbies, from photography to model planes to computer programming.

As Frank rolled the ball toward Chet, Chet drew his foot back and let loose a monster of a kick. He connected, and the ball went flying over Frank's head. No one was more surprised than Chet, who just stared at the soaring ball in open-mouthed surprise.

Joe let out a whoop. "Run, Chet!" he cried as he started for third base.

Iola sprinted after the ball. Chet had kicked it far, but she was fast. Joe rounded third and sprinted on to home plate. They were tied! Chet was almost at second base. If he could make it home before Iola tagged him out, they would win!

Chet was running with all his might, and so was Iola. She scooped up the ball just as Chet laid a hand on the oak tree that was third base. He kept sprinting, headed for home plate, and Joe could see a triumphant smile starting to spread across his mouth. He was going to make it!

But then Joe saw Iola coming up behind Chet—*fast*. It was going to be close!

Chet lunged for home plate just as Iola lunged for him, touching the ball to his back. Chet threw his hands up in the air and cheered.

"I'm safe!" he said, jumping up and down. "We won!"

"No way!" Iola said. "I tagged you out."

Chet shook his head. "You tagged me *after* I touched the base."

Joe looked at his brother. He wasn't sure which one was right, and judging by Frank's shrug, Frank wasn't either.

"Don't be a sore loser, Chet," Iola teased. "I tagged you before you touched the base, and you know it!"

"I'm not the sore loser. *You* are," Chet said. "Why do you always have to be the best at everything, Iola? I won fair and square!"

"Nuh-uh!" Iola stomped her foot.

"You're being a baby about this." Chet looked down at his watch. "Come on, we have to go home."

Iola stomped out of the yard and back in the direction of their house.

Chet sighed. "Sorry, guys."

"That's okay," Joe said. He didn't like to see Chet and Iola fight. He and Frank hardly *ever* fought.

"I'll see you at school tomorrow," Chet said as he started to go after his sister. "Let me know if you need any help with your case!"

BEWARE THE PHANTOM

"What's going on?" Frank said to his brother as they walked through the front doors of Bayport Elementary the next morning. The halls were full of kids standing around in groups, talking excitedly and all holding copies of the school newspaper.

Frank spotted Speedy in the hallway. Like everyone else, she was reading. He went up to her, Joe following behind him, and tapped her shoulder.

"Oh, hey, Frank!" she said. "Have you seen this?"

She handed him what she'd been reading. It was a copy of the *BES Gazette*, the school's newspaper. The headline was printed in big, bold letters:

THE PHANTOM OF THE TALENT SHOW: MYSTERY PRANKSTER STRIKES SCHOOL PRODUCTION

Frank quickly read Diego Mendez's article, while Joe leaned over his shoulder and read along with him.

> Rehearsal for the annual Bayport Elementary Talent Show was going great. The musical numbers by the student director from Bayport Middle School, eighth grader Olivia Shapiro, have taken an already wonderful show to a new level. But nothing could prepare me for the, well, unusual performance of Daniel Tate on the trumpet.

Diego wrote about the bubbles bursting out of
Daniel's trumpet and the hunt everyone had gone
on to find the person behind the prank. Then he
described the note they'd found in Daniel's instrument case, which promised more pranks if the talent
show wasn't canceled.

Will the Phantom of the Talent Show strike again? All I know for sure is that I'll be watching, and you should too. Tickets to the show can be reserved on the school's website or by calling the head office. Better get yours soon!

Well, Frank thought, *that* part would make Olivia happy. She was desperate for the show to sell out.

"Who do you think the Phantom is?" Speedy asked. "You two must have a theory."

All around them Frank could hear other students asking one another the same question. Who could it be? Who would want to stop the talent show?

"Maybe it's Adam Ackerman," Speedy continued. "Ellie said he was hanging around rehearsal the other day, and he told her he hoped the show was a disaster."

"That's true. I heard him," Joe said. "He was really mad. Ellie said he tried out for the show but didn't make it."

"He did," Frank said. As part of his job as the Backstage Buddy to the stage manager, he had been at the auditions. "He came in and just joked around on the stage for a few minutes. Mrs. Castle said he could only be in the show if he prepared a real act. She offered him a second chance to audition, but he never came back."

"If anyone was going to do something as mean as trying to get the talent show canceled," Speedy said, "it would be Adam."

It was almost time for school to start, so everyone said good-bye and headed toward their classrooms. The Phantom was all that anyone could talk about all day. Adam Ackerman was the most popular suspect, probably because of his reputation as Bayport Elementary's biggest bully.

Joe told Frank he had a different idea, though.

"Adam does have a good reason to want the talent show canceled," Joe said as they sat down to eat lunch together, "but he's not the only one."

"Yeah?" Frank asked.

Joe nodded as he took a huge bite from the

PB&J sandwich their mom had packed for him. When he spoke again, the words were muddled by the peanut butter in his mouth. "I think the Phantom might be Ezra."

"Really?" Frank was surprised. He didn't know Ezra very well, but he seemed really cool. He didn't seem like the type of person who would try to ruin a talent show.

Joe nodded. "I know he's a lot nicer than Adam, but he's dreading the show. His parents are making him do it, and he's afraid he'll get made fun of once everyone knows he plays the violin. There's no one on the *planet* who would be happier if the show was canceled. Not even Adam Ackerman."

Frank thought about that while he took out the notebook to write their next suspect down.

"That does make sense," he said. "And it would have been a lot easier for Ezra to pour the bubbles in Daniel's trumpet, since he would have been in that area anyway. Everyone knows Adam isn't supposed to be there, so he would have had to be a lot sneakier to get it done without anyone noticing."

"We should talk to both of them and see if we can learn anything," Joe said.

Frank nodded. "I'll take Adam. You take Ezra."

"Deal."

After lunch, Frank spotted Adam in the hall as he was walking back to his classroom. It wasn't hard, since Adam was the biggest person in their grade and stood almost a head taller than everyone else. Frank ran to catch up with him.

"Hey, Adam!" he said.

Adam spun to face Frank, his usual scowl firmly in place.

"I'm not the Phantom, okay?" he said. "Whoever he is, I owe him a high five, but it's not me."

"Well, where *were* you yesterday afternoon?" Frank asked.

Adam crossed his arms over his chest. "Detention."

"So you were in the school after classes ended?" Frank asked. "While the rehearsal was going on?"

"Yes, but I didn't do anything," Adam said. "Not that I expect you to believe me."

Frank frowned. Adam had a good "why" to be the Phantom: he'd said he wanted the show to be a disaster. *Plus*, he'd been in the school when the bubbles were poured into Daniel's trumpet. But Frank had the feeling that Adam was telling the truth, so he wasn't sure what to believe.

If it wasn't Adam, could the culprit be Ezra?

SOUR NOTES

Joe wasn't having any more luck cracking the case than Frank. Rehearsal had already started, and he still hadn't found a good way to ask Ezra if he was the Phantom.

"So, Ezra, did you read the article in the school paper?" Joe asked as they sat together in the green-room.

"Of course. It's all anyone's talked about today," Ezra said. "Pretty crazy, huh?"

"Yeah," Joe replied. "Did you see anything? In the hallway where Daniel left his trumpet case?"

Ezra shook his head. "I came straight here to the greenroom after the opening number. I was still here when Mrs. Castle canceled the rehearsal because of the Phantom."

"You didn't leave the greenroom during the break?" Joe asked.

Ezra shook his head.

Joe frowned. It sounded like Ezra had an alibi. If he was in the greenroom the whole time like he said, he *couldn't* be the Phantom.

"I'm going to go get a drink of water," Joe said. "I'll be right back."

On his way out of the classroom, Joe stopped to talk to Ellie Freeman, who was stationed at the door with her walkie-talkie.

"Hey, Ellie," he said.

"Hiya, Joe."

"Can I ask you a question?"

"Sure."

"Do you remember if Ezra left this room at all during yesterday's rehearsal?" Joe asked. "He says he was in here the whole time after the first number."

Ellie pursed her lips as she thought, but after a second she shrugged. "I'm really not sure. So many people come in and out that it's hard to keep track. Are you and Frank investigating this Phantom thing?"

"Just let me know if you remember anything weird about yesterday, would you?" Joe asked.

"You bet. I hope you figure out who it is!"

Joe walked into the hallway where Daniel had left his trumpet to check it out. It was a good spot for a prank, since it was usually empty during rehearsals. Joe decided he would walk from there to the backstage to see how long it would take. He needed all the information he could get if he was going to get to the bottom of this.

Joe walked from the spot the trumpet case had been toward the backstage at a normal pace, counting the seconds in his head. He went through the door to the backstage area and walked toward where Speedy stood just offstage. It was dark back there, the area lit by just one small blue lamp. He reached Speedy as she sent Iola out onto the stage for her song.

"Hi, Joe," Speedy whispered.

"Hey," he whispered back. "Mind if I watch for a minute?"

"No problem."

Joe peered around the black curtain that hid the backstage area from view. Iola was standing in the middle of the stage, a microphone in a stand placed in

front of her. Her shoulders were thrown back in con-
fidence, which made her look taller than she really
was. The opening strains of her song, "Tomorrow,"
began to play. Iola took a deep breath and leaned
into the microphone.

"The sun will come out . . . *RRRRRRRrrrribbit!*"

Iola jerked back from the microphone in shock.
After a moment, she swallowed and opened her
mouth again to sing.

"The . . . *Rrrrrrrribbit!*"

Once again, the frog sound croaked from the
speakers. All of a sudden, the backstage area was full of kids who had
heard the strange noise and come
running to see what had happened. Onstage, Iola was moving
her lips, but all anyone could
hear was the croaking of a
frog. Some kids were laughing, while others were whispering
to one another that the Phantom
had struck again.

Finally Iola ran offstage crying.

Joe heard Chet shout, "Iola! Wait!"

Then Olivia cried, "Stop the show! Everyone back to the greenroom!"

The kids backstage turned and scattered. Joe wasn't going to go back to the greenroom, though. He needed to investigate, so he stepped out onto the stage.

"What are you doing?" Speedy asked him.

"There's no way Iola could have been making those noises," he said. With Speedy at his side, he examined the microphone. It looked normal, but . . .

Joe tapped the mic. It made no sound.

"It isn't on?" Speedy asked.

Joe shook his head. He looked out into the auditorium and spotted Frank. He had to tell him this.

The stage was only a couple of feet off the ground, so Joe hopped down and headed for his brother. Frank was in the back of the auditorium in the sound area.

"Hey, Joe," Frank said when he saw his brother coming. "I'm starting to think this Phantom means business."

"I think you're right," Joe said. "The microphone on the stage isn't turned on. Wherever that croaking sound came from, it wasn't from Iola."

Frank frowned and went over to the sound equipment.

"Where's Chet?" Joe asked. Chet was in charge of running the sound for the show.

"He went after Iola when she ran away," Frank said. "He looked really worried."

Frank pressed a button and a CD tray slid open. Inside was a CD that was labeled *"Tomorrow" Music Track: Iola Morton*. Frank pushed the CD back in and let it play for a moment. There was no croaking. He pushed a couple of other buttons, and another CD tray opened.

He and Joe examined the CD that was in the second tray. It was a plain silver CD, and it had no label.

"Let's see what we've got," Frank said as he put the CD back into the player. He pressed play and the auditorium was filled with the sounds of "Tomorrow." The brothers looked at each other in confusion. Why were there two CDs with Iola's music track on them?

Then the croaking started.

"Someone made a copy of Iola's music and added croaking noises to it," Frank said. "They turned off the microphone so it would look like *she* was the one making the sound."

Joe didn't like what he was thinking. The music on the CDs, the microphone, all of that was part of the sound for the show. And the person in charge of the sound was . . .

Chet.

Chapter 7

FRIEND OR PHANTOM?

"I know what you're thinking," Frank said, "but it *couldn't* have been Chet. He would never try to ruin his sister's act . . . right?"

"It sure doesn't seem like Chet," Joe said, "but, well, they did get into that big fight yesterday. Maybe Chet was angrier than we thought."

Frank thought about that. If it were anyone else, it would seem like a good "why." But he had a hard time believing their friend could be the Phantom.

⮐ 279

"Let's go find him," Frank said.

He and Joe searched the halls for Chet and eventually found him leaning against the wall outside the girls' restroom.

"Hey, Chet," Frank said. "Did you find Iola?"

Chet nodded. "I finally got her to stop crying, but she's pretty upset. She's washing her face."

"Poor Iola!" Joe said.

"She'll be okay. She's just embarrassed," Chet said, "and confused. She has no idea what happened."

"Well, we figured out that part, at least," Frank said. "Someone made a copy of her music that had croaking on it, and her microphone was turned off. It only *looked* like she was making those sounds."

Chet's eyes went wide. "Oh, man. I'm helping with the music and the microphones. I should have noticed something was wrong!"

"But . . ." Joe trailed off. He looked at Frank and then back at Chet. "But you didn't do anything, right?"

"Of course not!" Chet said, angry. "She's my *sister*.

I tease her a lot, but I would never try to mess up her act or the show!"

"We know you wouldn't," Frank said. He felt bad for suspecting Chet for even a second. Of course he wasn't the Phantom! "When Iola comes out, tell her we're going to find out who did this."

"Thanks, guys," Chet said. "Would you mind helping me with something else?"

"Sure, Chet," Frank said.

"Anything you want," Joe added.

"I want to do something nice for Iola," Chet explained. "Not just because of this, but because of that fight we had yesterday. She drives me crazy sometimes, but she's a really good sister. I have an idea that might make her feel better."

The next morning Frank, Joe, and Chet arrived at school early, long before any other students. Chet's backpack was full of their supplies, and Frank carried a white posterboard. They spent the rest of the time before school decorating a poster. They taped up sparkly letters that spelled out her name, pictures of her favorite band and baseball players cut from magazines, and little notes that said things like *Iola rocks!* and *We ♥ Iola*. They finished decorating the poster just as other students started to arrive. They hid around a corner holding the poster to see Iola's reaction when she discovered their surprise.

A couple of minutes later, Frank spotted Iola coming down the hall and elbowed the other boys. They grinned as they jumped out and saw her smile when she saw the decorated board.

"Surprise!" the boys cried.

"Oh, guys, this is awesome!" Iola gushed. "I love it!"

"It was Chet's idea," Frank said. "Joe and I just helped."

Iola gave Chet a big hug. "You're the best brother in the whole world."

Chet's cheeks turned pink, and he rubbed the back of his neck. "Well, I try."

"We're going to double- and triple-check your music today, Iola," Frank said. "The Phantom's not going to get you again. You're going to be great."

"Thanks, you guys," Iola said.

"Hey!"

They all turned their heads in the direction of the shriek that came from the other end of the hall. It was their friend Ellie Freeman. She was pointing at a poster for the talent show that was hung on the wall.

"Who did this?" Ellie demanded.

Frank and Joe rushed to check it out. Someone had scribbled all over the poster in a fat red marker.

Speedy ran up to them with another poster in her hand. It, too, had a note from the Phantom written on it.

"The Phantom did this to every poster in the whole school!" she said.

Frank turned to his brother. "We were the first ones in the school today," he said. "We would have seen someone messing with the posters."

Joe nodded. "Whoever it was, they must have done it yesterday after school."

"You're right," Frank said. "That means the Phantom is *definitely* someone involved with the talent show."

A SLIMY SURPRISE

It was the final dress rehearsal. The talent show was the next night, and everyone was excited and nervous. The Phantom wanted to get the talent show canceled, and this rehearsal was his or her last chance. Everyone was holding their breath to see what the Phantom might do. Diego Mendez was there to see if the Phantom would strike again. The school paper was putting out a special issue on the talent show and the Phantom the next morning.

Olivia called the entire cast into the auditorium. She handed over her notes to Zoe—things like *Remember to smile* and *Keep your head up*—while she went to the restroom. While Zoe was reading, Joe snuck to the back of the auditorium, where Frank was going over his checklists.

"Hey, bro," he said. "I've been thinking."

"Oh yeah? Did it hurt?" Frank teased.

Joe smiled and rolled his eyes. "Ha-ha. Anyway, I was thinking I should hang out backstage during the rehearsal today instead of in the greenroom. If the Phantom tries something, I'll have a better chance of catching them."

Frank nodded. "That's a good idea. I'll tell Speedy you'll be back there."

Olivia returned, hands stuck in her pockets, just as Zoe finished reading her notes. Zoe tried to hand the notebook back to her, but Olivia shook her head.

"I want you to write down the notes for me today," she told Zoe. Then she turned to the cast. "Okay, everyone! Places for the start of the show, please!"

After performing in the first number with the rest of the cast, Joe took his spot backstage near Speedy while the other kids went to the green-room. From there he could see what was going on onstage as well as the table full of props that sat in the wings. The balls and fake rubber knives he was going to juggle were there, along with instruments, magic tricks, costume hats, and other items. No one would be able to mess with any of them without Joe seeing it.

Joe could tell that a lot of the kids were nervous as they went out onstage. As the show continued and there was no sign of the Phantom, everyone started to relax a little. Frank and the rest of the Backstage Buddy crew worked like a well-oiled machine, and even Olivia seemed happy with the way things were going. Joe's juggling act went perfectly; he didn't drop a single thing.

Annie Norland, Desiree Perry, and Lauren Brenner were the next-to-last act of the show. They were doing a dance number together. The three girls walked up to the props table where they kept the bowler hats they wore for most of their dance. The hats were hot and itchy, so they never put them on until the last minute.

"Break a leg!" Joe whispered as they got ready to go onstage.

All three girls turned and stared at him.

"Oops," he said. "That's probably not the right thing to say to dancers, is it?"

Annie grinned. "It's okay. We know what you meant."

Onstage, the lights went down.

"Okay, ladies," Speedy said. "Time to go!"

Annie, Desiree, and Lauren walked out onto the stage and struck a pose. The lights came up on them, their music started to play, and they began to dance. Joe wondered why the Phantom hadn't struck that day. Maybe whoever it was had given up, or maybe they hadn't been able to perform their prank because of Joe standing guard over the props table.

Joe watched the girls dancing. If he had to guess, he'd bet they were going to be the crowd favorite. His favorite part of their act was coming up: the moment when they took off their hats and shook out their hair as the music got really loud and crazy. Joe inched closer to the stage so he'd have a better view.

The girls took off their hats, and Desiree shook out her long black hair while Lauren whipped her auburn curls around her face. But when Annie spun, instead of her blond hair flying behind her, huge globs of green slime started going everywhere!

Onstage, Desiree caught a glimpse of Annie's hair and shrieked. Lauren froze and stared at her friend.

"Stop!" Olivia shouted over the music. "Stop the show!"

"What is it?" Annie asked, looking at her dumbstruck friends.

"Annie, your—your hair!" Desiree stammered, pointing to her friend's head.

Annie grabbed a handful of her hair and held it up to her eyes. When she saw the electric green color, she screamed.

"What *is* that?" she screeched. "Get it out of my hair!"

Joe rushed onto the stage just as Annie rushed off, followed by her friends. He gathered up the hats the girls had dropped and was already examining them when Frank got there. One of the hats had a layer of thick green slime smeared on the inside of it.

"Someone put that green goop in the hat," Joe explained to Frank, showing him what he'd found. "I don't know how they did it. I was backstage next to the prop table the entire time."

"The Phantom must have done it before you started standing there," Frank said. "Either that, or the person who's doing this really *is* a phantom."

Olivia appeared on the stage, with Zoe and Diego following her. Diego's pencil was flying across his notebook. He would sure have an interesting story for tomorrow's special edition of the paper!

"Frank, get everyone on the stage, please," Olivia said. "I need to talk to them."

Frank got on the radio to give the message to the backstage crew, and together they gathered the cast onstage. The last people to arrive were Annie, Desiree, and Lauren. Annie had been trying to wash the slime out of her hair in the girls' restroom with her friends' help. Her wet hair was dripping water down the back of her costume, and it still looked pretty green to Joe.

"This was stuck to the bathroom mirror," she told everyone. Annie held up a small piece of paper. "It says 'Cancel the talent show or this won't be the last you hear from me. Love, the Phantom.'"

Chapter 9

IN THE SPOTLIGHT

It was Friday, and almost time for the show to begin. The auditorium was packed with people. Not only was every seat sold out, but there was a row of people standing in the back. The entire school had turned up to see the show because of Diego's articles about the Phantom.

Olivia was the happiest Frank had ever seen her. The two of them were overseeing last-minute preparations backstage. Frank was dressed all in black, just like the rest of the Backstage Buddy crew, while Olivia was wearing a sparkly pink dress with elbow-length white gloves. Frank thought it was weird that Olivia was wearing the long gloves, but then again, most of the things Olivia wore seemed weird to Frank!

"This is extraordinary, Olivia," Mrs. Castle said. "I've never seen so many people in the audience for the talent show!"

Olivia beamed. "Thank you, Mrs. Castle."

Frank felt a tap on his shoulder and turned to find Speedy standing next to him.

"We have a problem, boss," she said. "Olivia should probably come too."

Frank grabbed Olivia, and the two of them followed Speedy to the greenroom where the cast, in lots of colorful costumes, was waiting for the show to begin.

"What's going on?" Olivia asked.

"They're scared," Speedy said. "They don't want to do the show."

A boy in a tuxedo jacket and top hat said, "What if the Phantom does something?"

A girl in a silver leotard who had her arm around her friend nodded. "Yeah, what if the Phantom makes something go wrong with my act and everyone out there laughs at me?"

"We should just cancel the show like the Phantom says," someone else shouted.

More and more kids started to chime in, until the room was full of noise. Olivia tried to shush them, but no one could hear her over all the talking. Finally, she stood on a chair, stuck two fingers in her mouth, and let out an ear-piercing whistle that made everyone freeze.

"Listen up, everybody!" Olivia said. "There's a saying in show business: 'The show must go on.' If we cancel the talent show, the Phantom wins. Does anyone want that?"

Everyone in the cast shook their heads.

"You all are too talented and you've worked too hard to give up now," she continued. "The only way we can beat the Phantom is by going ahead with the show and doing the best job we can. Right?"

The kids looked at one another and started to nod.

"This auditorium is packed with people who want to see you perform, and I know we can give them an *amazing* show," Olivia said. She pointed at the boy in the tuxedo and top hat. "Will, don't you want your classmates to see how great you are at magic?"

Will nodded. "Yeah."

"And Iola," Olivia said. "Don't you want your parents to hear you sing?"

Iola stood. "You bet I do!"

"You're all going to be incredible tonight," Olivia said, "so let's get out there and give that audience the best show they've ever seen!"

"Yeah!" the cast cheered.

"Great!" Olivia said. "Now, get to your places for the opening number, and let's have a great show!"

The cast gave each other high fives and pats on the back as they walked to their places. Frank stayed behind to talk to Speedy for a minute, and when he headed toward the auditorium to take his place, he spotted Ezra Moore talking to Olivia. Ezra was one of Joe's top suspects, so Frank walked extra slowly past the two of them and kept his ears open.

"Please, Olivia," Ezra said. "Don't make me go out there."

"You're going to do this, Ezra," Olivia said. "I've done *everything* I could to make this the best talent show ever, and you're not going to ruin it for me."

Frank's attention was so focused on listening to the conversation that he didn't notice Annie Norland until he bumped right into her.

"Oops! Sorry, Annie!" he said.

"That's okay," she said. "No harm done."

"Hey," he added, looking at the long blond hair falling over her shoulders. "It looks like all the green came out of your hair!"

She laughed. "Yeah, I only had to wash it seven times. Look at this, though." She bent down to show him the top of her head. The skin beneath her hair was still pretty green. "It came out of my hair, but I guess the color in that slime takes longer to wash off skin."

"Well, at least no one can see it," Frank said. "Make sure you check your hat before you put it on tonight, okay?"

She smiled. "You bet I will. Have a good show, Frank."

"You too," Frank said.

He made his way to the small desk that Mrs. Castle had set up for him in the back of the auditorium. It had a tiny reading light that he could use to read his checklists and his notebook, where he'd written down all the instructions for the show.

Frank's heart was beating fast in his chest from excitement and a little bit of nervousness. He wasn't thinking about the Phantom anymore, just the job in front of him.

Frank got on the radio and checked in with the crew. Speedy told him that everyone was in place backstage and ready to go. Chet and Eli both assured him that they were ready with the right music and lights. Soon after, Olivia came to check in with him.

"Are we ready?" she asked. "It's almost time."

"We're ready when you are," he said.

"I want to thank you, Frank. You've been an excellent BBB stage manager." She gave him her gloved hand to shake. "I'm sure you're going to do a great job tonight."

"Thanks, Olivia," he said. He found himself staring at those odd elbow-length gloves Olivia was wearing as he shook her hand.

"Okay, Frank," she said. "Start the show."

Frank nodded and got on the radio. "Here we go, everybody!"

The lights went down in the auditorium, and

the sold-out audience began to clap and cheer as the curtain rose and the music swelled. Kids spilled onto the stage. The show had started. Olivia clapped her gloved hands in excitement next to Frank.

All of a sudden, it hit Frank like a bolt of lightning. He knew who the Phantom was!

Do you?

THE HARDY BOYS—and
YOU!

CAN YOU SOLVE THE MYSTERY OF THE TALENT SHOW TRICKS?

Grab a piece of paper and write your answers down.
Or just turn the page to find out!

1. Frank and Joe came up with a list of suspects.
   Can you think of more? Who do you think
   is playing the tricks on the talent show acts?

2. Which clues helped you to solve this mystery?
   Write them down.

THE GRAND FINALE

Joe and the rest of the cast ran off the stage with giant grins on their faces. The show had just ended, and it had gone perfectly. All their hard work in rehearsals had paid off, and they'd gotten a huge standing ovation from the sold-out audience. Even better than that, there'd been no sign of the Phantom.

Everyone hugged and gave each other high fives back in the greenroom. Joe stood up on a chair and shouted above the noise. "Hey, everybody! You were all awesome tonight! We pulled it off!"

The entire cast cheered, and the kids standing next to Ezra patted him on the back. A smile slowly spread across his face, and soon he was beaming more than anyone else. He had made it through the show!

Joe climbed down from the chair and went up to him. "You were great, Ezra. There's no *way* anyone's going to make fun of you after that."

Ezra nodded. "Thanks, Joe."

Joe went to where he'd left his backpack against the wall and started to put away his juggling props. He was zipping the bag closed when he felt a hand on his shoulder. He turned and found Frank standing there.

"Hey!" he said. "Good job tonight!"

"Thanks! You were great too. You didn't drop a single ball. I'm impressed," Frank joked.

"And *you* managed to keep the lights on for the whole show," Joe teased back.

"Listen." Frank stepped close to him and

dropped his voice low. "I think I know who the Phantom is."

"Really?" Joe said.

"Yeah. I was talking to Annie and—"

"Congratulations, ladies and gentlemen!" Olivia said as she and Mrs. Castle entered the greenroom together. "You were magnificent!"

"Yes, excellent job, everyone," Mrs. Castle said. "As a reward for all your hard work, we have a little surprise for you. Pizza party in the music room!"

Everyone cheered and followed Mrs. Castle to her classroom. Boxes of all kinds of pizza, bottles of soda, and a plate full of cupcakes were waiting for them. Joe ran to get a plate before all the pepperoni was gone. He sat down with Speedy, Chet, and Iola and dug into his slice.

It wasn't until Frank sat down beside him that Joe remembered. The Phantom! The idea of pizza had completely made him forget that his brother thought he knew who the Phantom was. He must have been even hungrier than usual.

Joe nudged his brother. "So, about what you were saying before?"

"Oh, right," Frank said. "Well, there's just one thing I need to check before I'm completely, one hundred percent sure. Hand me your cup."

Joe handed over his empty plastic cup and watched his brother as he stood and walked to the table of soda bottles. He poured a full cup of cola and started to walk back. Halfway there, he tripped over his own feet and "accidentally" poured the cup of soda all over Olivia.

"Ahhhhh!" Olivia squealed. "Watch what you're doing!"

"Oops!" Frank said. "I'm sorry!"

Zoe ran to get a stack of napkins and started to dab at Olivia's white gloves, which were covered with the brown cola.

"It'll be okay!" Zoe said. "Take these gloves off, and I'll go wash them in the sink."

"No, it's fine," Olivia said quickly. "Don't worry about it."

"Don't be silly," Zoe insisted. "You're going to be all wet and sticky."

"I don't mind!" Olivia snapped.

"It will only take a minute!" Zoe said, and she pulled off one of Olivia's long gloves.

Joe stared.

Olivia's hands were stained a bright neon green.

"Hey," Annie said, looking up from her conversation with Desiree and Lauren. "Olivia, why are your fingers green?"

"What?" Olivia stammered. "I—uh—I don't—"

She tried to hide her hand, but her dress didn't have any pockets. It was too late anyway. Too many people had already seen her green fingers.

"Your fingers!" Annie exclaimed, jumping to her feet. "They're stained the same color as that slime the Phantom put in my hat!"

Olivia's face was pale.

"Wait—are *you* the Phantom?" Annie asked.

"Olivia," Mrs. Castle asked, a worried expression on her face. "What's going on here?"

"Okay, fine, it was me!" Olivia burst out. She pointed at Annie. "I put that stupid green gooey stuff in your hat and put the bubbles in Daniel's trumpet and made it seem like Iola was croaking! But I did it for all of *you*. I just wanted this to be the biggest, best talent show ever, and . . . and . . ."

"And you knew that articles in the school newspaper about the 'Phantom of the Talent Show' would get the whole school excited for the show," Frank finished. "You were scared that tickets weren't selling fast enough, and you needed to do something to make sure the show was a success."

"It worked, didn't it?" Olivia pointed out. "That was the biggest audience the talent show has ever had!"

Mrs. Castle shook her head. "Olivia, you should have known better," she scolded. "That's not the mark of a good director!"

Olivia looked down at the floor.

"I'm sorry, guys," she said softly. "I didn't mean to scare anyone or ruin your hair, Annie! I just wanted people to see our show."

Annie's frown slowly disappeared, and she sighed. "Well, the green is already washing out. I'm still kind of mad, but I forgive you, Olivia."

"Yeah, me too," Daniel said.

"And me," Iola piped up.

Olivia gave Annie a big hug. "Oh, thank you. I really am sorry. I know I got carried away this time. Mrs. Castle, I'll accept whatever punishment you think I deserve."

Mrs. Castle put a hand on Olivia's shoulder. "We can talk about that on Monday. For now, let's all just enjoy the party."

The cast and crew finished their pizza and cupcakes, and then they all waved good-bye to one another as they went home with their parents.

"I can't believe Olivia did that," Frank said. He and Joe were heading out to their tree house after the party.

"She was always a little dramatic, but I didn't

think she would try to ruin the show," Joe added. "At least she was sorry about everything."

The boys climbed up to the tree house, using their flashlights to guide the way.

With big grins, Joe and Frank gave each other a high five as they settled in for a fun tree house sleepover.

FOLLOW THE TRAIL AND SOLVE MYSTERIES WITH FRANK AND JOE

HardyBoysSeries.com

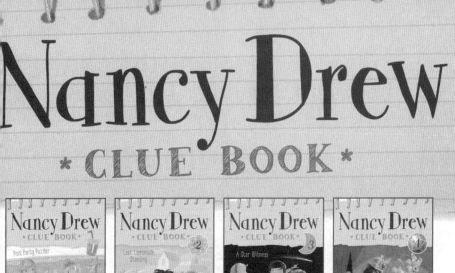

Nancy Drew
★ CLUE BOOK ★

Test your detective skills with Nancy and her best friends, Bess and George!

NancyDrew.com

EBOOK EDITIONS ALSO AVAILABLE
From Aladdin ★ simonandschuster.com/kids